For Dalton's plan to work, he had to make everyone else think he and Sydney were a couple.

If he was to keep her safe, he had no other choice.

"Syd?" he whispered.

"Uh-huh?"

He sensed she was feeling a little buzzed from the champagne. Good, maybe she wouldn't nail him with a karate kick after what he was about to do.

"I'm sorry," he said. "But I'm going to have to kiss you."

She straightened, but before she could protest he cupped her chin between his forefinger and thumb.

Tipped her head.

And tasted the most amazing girl he'd ever kissed.

PAT
WHITE

RENEGADE
SOLDIER

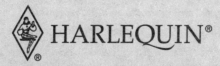

HARLEQUIN®

TORONTO • NEW YORK • LONDON
AMSTERDAM • PARIS • SYDNEY • HAMBURG
STOCKHOLM • ATHENS • TOKYO • MILAN • MADRID
PRAGUE • WARSAW • BUDAPEST • AUCKLAND

To Margaret Watson, for your friendship and inspiration.

Recycling programs
for this product may
not exist in your area.

ISBN-13: 978-0-373-69386-3
ISBN-10:   0-373-69386-9

RENEGADE SOLDIER

Copyright © 2009 by Pat White

www.eHarlequin.com

Printed in U.S.A.

ABOUT THE AUTHOR

Growing up in the Midwest, Pat White has been spinning stories in her head ever since she was a little girl—stories filled with mystery, romance and adventure. Years later, while trying to solve the mysteries of raising a family in a house full of men, she started writing romance fiction. After six Golden Heart nominations and a *Romantic Times BOOKreviews* Award for Best Contemporary Romance (2004), her passion for storytelling and love of a good romance continues to find a voice in her tales of romantic suspense. Pat now lives in the Pacific Northwest and she's still trying to solve the mysteries of living in a house full of men—with the added complication of two silly dogs and three spoiled cats. She loves to hear from readers, so please visit her at www.patwhitebooks.com.

Books by Pat White

HARLEQUIN INTRIGUE

*The Blackwell Group
†Assignment: The Girl Next Door

CAST OF CHARACTERS

Dalton Keen—AW-21 agent whose brother, Nate, goes missing after helping Dalton with an assignment.

Sydney Trent—Locke, Inc. administrative assistant and Nate's best friend. Syd dreams of traveling the world after spending years taking care of her sick parents.

Nathaniel Keen—Naive and trusting, the Locke, Inc. computer genius stumbles onto something peculiar at work.

Arthur Locke—Founder of the multibillion-dollar company that, among other things, provides information systems security to businesses and select government agencies.

Stewart Pratt—Locke's right-hand man. His goal is to coerce Nate into helping them with a dangerous project.

AW-21—Covert branch of the National Security Agency designed to defend the United States against terrorism.

Chapter One

Dalton Keen's future would be determined in the next ten minutes.

Leaning against the metal railing at Seattle's Pier 69, he eyed the vessel that had just brought hundreds of passengers in from Canada—one of them a suspected terrorist.

By helping apprehend the suspect, Dalton hoped to earn his way back into the field. He was ready; he'd been ready for months. But as an agent for AW-21, a covert branch of the NSA, he was at the mercy of rules and regulations: traumatized agents were not to be sent back into the field prematurely. Instead, agents were sent to Port Townsend, a remote town in Washington State, not far from Seattle.

Traumatized? More like pissed off. Dalton had trusted the wrong person and nearly got himself, and the hostage, killed on the mission in Syria. Trust was not a mistake Dalton would make again.

"The vessel is docked," lead agent Zack Carter said into Dalton's earpiece. "You in position?"

"Affirmative, sir." Dalton's job was to be inconspicuous and offer support when Carter apprehended the suspect.

Hell, Dalton was anxious to resume duties rescuing hostages or breaking into secure compounds to retrieve critical intelligence. He'd forced his way into the microchip case hoping to impress C.O. Andrews and earn a spot back on the A team.

His good work didn't get him back into the field, at least not yet, but it did aggravate his already tenuous relationship with his brother, Nate.

"Do you have a visual of the passengers?" Carter asked.

"Yes, sir. They are disembarking the vessel, waiting in line to go through customs."

Carter had positioned himself inside the building. He'd identify the suspect to a customs officer who would casually pull him aside. The senior agent was a pro, and probably wouldn't even need Dalton's help.

But Dalton had needed Nate's. He'd asked his genius brother for help with the microchip case thinking it might bridge the gap between them, while earning Dalton points. Nate had come through, making Dalton look like a hero to his superior officer.

Only, baby brother wouldn't let it go. He kept rambling about a conspiracy at his work, Locke, Inc., an Internet security giant that had contracts with both the private and public sectors.

The kid just wanted to feel important. He'd always been desperate to receive as much attention as Dalton, the charming athlete-turned-war-hero.

Hero, my ass.

Dalton had hoped that needing Nate's help might destroy his hero worship. If anyone should be doing the worship routine, it should be Dalton worshipping his eccentric, brilliant little brother.

Brilliant, but lacking in common sense. Everything was a game to Nate. He continued to theorize about the microchip ID number, claiming it resembled a number he'd seen on a chip at work.

At which point Dalton started to wonder if Nate was suffering from schizophrenia. Brilliant people often struggled with the disease.

The tourists weren't going to be released onto the streets of Seattle anytime soon. Dalton leaned against the rail and called his brother.

"This is Nate. Leave a message and I might call you back." Pause. "Or I might not."

BEEP.

"Little brother, it's been over a week and I haven't heard from you. I'm in Seattle tonight, it's Thursday, and I thought we could—"

"He's got a gun!" a woman screamed.

A stampede of frightened passengers rushed the customs building as a man waved a firearm in the air. Dalton pocketed his cell phone.

"Carter, there is an armed suspect on the gangplank. Permission to apprehend?"

"Negative. Hold your position."

"He's crazy. A crazy man is going to kill us!" another woman screamed.

Crazy, like Dalton's baby brother? His brilliance coupled with the mental abuse from their father could have sent him over the edge of sanity. And once again Dalton was too absorbed in his own life to see it coming.

"Keen, our suspect is six feet, a hundred and forty—"

The radio went dead.

"Carter?"

Dalton held his position and eyed the group fleeing the building. Four Seattle PD cruisers pulled up, blocking Alaskan Way to get control of the situation.

Dalton glanced at the fruitcake waving a gun, then back at the cops. "Hurry up, damn it," he muttered.

The cops struggled to get through the mass of panicked tourists.

"Let me go!"

Dalton snapped his attention to the boat where the gun-wielding idiot was dragging a kid, maybe fifteen years old, back toward the vessel.

"Mom!" the kid cried.

The woman, who Dalton assumed was the mother, stood there with a blank look on her face.

Say something.

"Mom!" the kid yelled again.

The gunman yanked the kid back. "Shut up!"

The boy was defenseless.

Like Nate had been.

"Screw this," Dalton muttered. He raced to the other end of the pier, climbed down and edged his way toward the cabin.

Hell, the cops weren't going to let any of these people leave without going through customs. Carter's suspect was either this bozo with a gun, which he doubted, or buried in the mass of people desperate to get away from the insanity.

Dalton sneaked onto the boat and eyed the main cabin through the window. The gunman shoved the kid into a cushioned seat and was ranting about something. When a cop stepped up to the doorway, the guy pointed his gun at the kid.

Not acceptable.

Dalton entered the cabin, pretending not to notice the assailant, as he searched between the seats as if looking for something.

"Get out!" the guy cried, pointing the gun at Dalton instead of the kid.

"Holy crap, dude. I'm sorry. I forgot my book."

Dalton eyed the cop and hoped the guy had enough sense to take an opportunity when presented.

"Get off my boat!" the crazy man hollered.

"No problem. Wait, there it is!" Dalton lunged for the floor and the lunatic fired at him. Dalton heard a grunt and a thud.

"I got him!" the policeman said.

Dalton stood and another cop pointed his firearm at him.

"No, he's okay," said the cop who'd tackled the nutcase.

"Keen, I've apprehended the suspect," Carter said. "We'll meet you out front."

"Yes, sir."

"What?" the second cop asked.

Dalton tapped his earpiece. "I'm NSA." He flashed his badge. "I've got to get to the street level ASAP."

The cop waved him on.

"Hey, thanks," the first cop said, kneeling on the nutcase's back and cuffing him.

"Sure." Dalton glanced at the kid and smiled, then high tailed it back to the pier. He leaned against the rail, trying to slow his breathing and calm the adrenaline rush of being target practice. Carter approached, escorting a middle-aged, skinny guy.

"You okay?" Carter inquired.

"Yes, sir."

Carter glanced at the cops taking the gunman off the boat, then back at Dalton. "Get the car, soldier."

"Yes, sir."

As Dalton raced to the nearby lot, his cell vibrated. The caller ID was restricted. Dalton hoped to God it was Nate.

"Keen," he answered.

"This is Commanding Officer Andrews. Carter isn't answering his phone. Did you apprehend the suspect?"

"Yes, sir."

"Your support on this project, and the microchip case has convinced me that you are field-ready, Keen."

"Thank you, sir." Hallelujah!

"Be ready to ship out."

"Yes, sir."

Dalton got into the SUV and nearly shouted in celebration. Back into the field. Outstanding.

Then the terrified face of the teenager drifted across his thoughts. The kid reminded him of Nate. Dalton didn't want to leave the Seattle area without resolving the tension between them.

Whether Nate was avoiding Dalton due to hurt feelings, or he was suffering from a mental disease, Dalton needed to find him and put things right. And he needed to complete that mission ASAP.

COWERING IN THE ALLEY beside a Dumpster, Nate clung to the laptop with trembling fingers.

He needed help. He needed Dalton.

That's it, run to big brother, you wuss. No, he had to do this by himself. Yet he didn't have the Special Ops training or the brute strength of his athletic brother.

But you have intelligence.

He fought back the panic that threatened to shut him down like a faulty hard drive. He'd stumbled onto something peculiar at work and had created a file. But when he'd tried to talk to his brother about it, Dalton dismissed Nate's excitement.

Nate wished his theory was wrong, but the fact he was being hunted in the alleys of Seattle proved that he'd discovered something he shouldn't have. And the microchip ID number had been the final clue. The chip had been produced by one of Locke's subsidiaries in Turkey—a chip designed to be used as a weapon against the United States.

"Need to keep moving," he whispered, pushing up against

the wall. At this point he could hardly focus on anything but the fear pounding in his chest.

He was twenty-eight and he was going to die. And that wasn't the worst of it. Others would die because he'd discovered the plan but was too weak to do anything about it.

Tonight, hiding in the dark alley, he wished he was a warrior like Dalton, not a computer geek coward.

"Over here!" a voice called.

Nate's body started to tremble uncontrollably.

"Dalton," he whispered to himself, his fingers tightening on the laptop. "What do I do?"

"HEY, ANGELA, I'M COVERING for lunch," Sydney Trent said, walking up to the main reception desk at Locke, Inc.

"Awesome, I'm starving." The phone buzzed and Angela picked up. "Good morning, Locke, Incorporated, Kirkland, Washington. Thank you." Angela punched in a number, ripped off the earpiece and shoved it at Syd. "It's all yours."

"Have a nice lunch," Syd said to the girl's back. It was obvious she didn't love her job. Well, get in line, neither did Syd, but the pay was decent and the benefits amazing. After three years of service, she was allowed to take a month's leave. She could hardly wait to take her first big trip next spring. Eventually, once she'd saved enough money, she'd take a whole year off to see the world.

After years of caring for two ailing parents, Syd's dream was within reach. Only, she'd hoped to travel with a companion, a boyfriend, or even her parents. But with their bad health and subsequent passing, Syd accepted that this dream would be experienced alone.

She slid behind the desk in the main reception area of Locke, Inc., with windows overlooking a particularly nice spot of Lake Washington, and glanced at boats sailing past.

She rarely got a good look outside from her post upstairs on the Technology floor.

She welcomed the break to cover for Angela, especially since she'd follow it with lunch by the Kirkland waterfront. It was during these small breaks from her busy administrative job that she fantasized about her trips.

With a sigh she glanced up at an intense-looking, determined man in his thirties coming toward her. He wore jeans, a tight T-shirt spanning a solid chest and dark sunglasses.

She hesitated before speaking, and it was at that moment she realized how out of practice she was interacting with gorgeous, powerful men. A cute girl like Syd didn't attract the gorgeous types.

Mr. Gorgeous with the short, brown hair and broad shoulders breezed past her and headed for the elevator as if she were invisible. Although he left her breathless, she had little effect on him.

"Excuse me, sir." She stood, her ego pricked. "You're not allowed up there."

When he didn't respond, she pressed the security button then chased after him. Locke, Inc. was strict about not letting outsiders into their offices since they dealt with security issues for major companies and the government.

"Sir," she said, hoping to keep him detained long enough for security to manage this situation. She rushed in front of the stranger. "You are not allowed upstairs."

He slid his sunglasses down the bridge of his nose and leveled her with the most amazing shade of blue-green eyes.

"Why not?" he asked.

It took her a second to process that he'd spoken to her. Oh, boy. Not good. She wished he'd come a few minutes earlier. Sexy Angela wouldn't have been fazed by this man's rugged good looks.

"It's company policy. Employees only." She steadied her breathing and motioned for him to join her back at the desk. He eyed her outfit, a mix of Goodwill stores' classic finds: a dark blue skirt, cream-colored cotton sweater and print scarf for added oomph. It was stylish, even if it didn't have a price tag of two hundred bucks.

Sitting behind the desk once again, she ignored his not-so-subtle analysis of her outfit. She leveled him with an irritated glare. "Do you have a problem?"

"No, no problem." He smiled.

Her body warmed.

And he winked.

The jerk knew he had some kind of magical power over her. Men like this were so darn irritating.

Rick, the security guard, approached the desk. "Is everything okay?"

"This gentleman was trying to go upstairs without authorization," she explained.

The stranger leaned over the desk. "You called security on me?"

"Step back, sir," Rick said. "Do you have business here?"

He continued to stare at Syd. "My name is Dalton Keen. My brother, Nate, works here."

She couldn't believe this bruiser was related to her absent-minded genius friend, a friend who referred to his older brother as a hero. Then it dawned on her why Nathaniel was so socially awkward: he'd grown up in this man's shadow.

"Is Nathaniel expecting you?" Syd asked, breaking eye contact and picking up the phone. But she knew Nathaniel wouldn't answer. She hadn't seen him in days and figured he was buried in some big project.

"Nathaniel?" Dalton asked.

She looked up.

"You know him?" he pushed.

She ignored the question. "I'll try his office."

The phone rang and she watched the security guard and Dalton size each other up. Rick placed his hand to the baton at his waist. Dalton leaned against the desk and smiled, as if challenging Rick to take a swing at him.

They were like a couple of four-year-olds poised over the biggest squirt gun.

Her call went into Nathaniel's voice mail.

She hung up. "I'm sorry, sir. Mr. Keen is not in the office. He might be at lunch."

"I was hoping to take him to lunch."

"Did you try his cell phone? If you're his brother, I'm sure you have that number." She was starting to sound rude but she wanted him to go away and let her refocus on straightening up Angela's desk. *Yeah, girl, that's not the only reason you want him out of your space.*

"*If* I'm his brother? You're calling me a liar?"

"I'm sorry if I've offended you. That was not my intent."

"Apology accepted." He fiddled with the nameplate. "Angela."

She didn't correct him and Rick shot her a questioning look. "I need to get back to work," she said, shuffling papers.

"May I escort you out, sir?" Rick said to Nate's bruiser big brother.

"Actually, I think I'll wait for Nate to return from lunch," Dalton said.

She aimed her pen toward the sofas across the lobby. "Make yourself comfortable. We have plenty of magazines to keep you occupied."

Of course, she didn't think he'd be into *Technology Today* or *Newsweek*. No, he was more of the *Playboy* kind of guy.

Rick escorted Dalton to the official waiting area. At first

she thought he'd sit with his back to her and gaze out onto Lake Washington. Instead, he shifted onto the sofa directly facing her. Wonderful, she'd be stuck looking at that handsome face for the next fifty minutes until Angela returned.

Rick hovered beside her desk. "You sure this is okay?"

"It's fine, thanks." She smiled and sifted through a stack of messages. A few of them were for Nathaniel and marked *Urgent.* Odd. The urgent messages were usually delivered right away by the mail-room staff. What were they doing here at reception?

"How well do you know him?" Dalton Keen's voice echoed across the granite floor.

She glanced up. "Excuse me?"

"My brother. How well do you know him?"

"We're friends."

"Impossible."

Voices from the past taunted her, the teasing and ridicule, thanks to her learning disability.

"Do you usually insult people you've just met?" she asked.

"Insult you?"

"You assume that because I'm obviously not as smart as your brother we couldn't possibly have anything in common and therefore couldn't be friends. I get it."

"No, what I meant was, I would find it impossible to be friends with an adorable girl like you."

"Yes, well, you are not your brother."

A call buzzed the switchboard. Saved!

She answered and forwarded the call. Dalton stood and glanced down the hall as if to make sure the security guard was gone.

He stepped closer to her desk. "Look, I sense you and I are meant to be fighters, not lovers, but can't you help me out? I'm worried. My kid brother can be a little naive and trusting."

"And that's a bad thing?" she challenged.

He shook his head. "Man, I can't win with you, can I? Look, I just want to make sure the kid's okay."

"Nathaniel is not a kid. He's a grown man and can take care of himself." She paused. "Most of the time."

He cocked his head and shot her a knowing look. "Wait a minute, you've got a crush on him?"

"It's not a crush. And you wouldn't understand."

Some days Syd wasn't sure she understood her relationship with Nathaniel, the computer genius with the kind soul. He'd worked his way into her heart right off when he'd saved her butt during her probation period. Nathaniel, the sweetheart, claimed he'd made the mistake that shipped vital computer software to the wrong location. He knew Locke, Inc. needed a man of his brilliance too much to fire him. He'd saved her job and she was eternally grateful.

Even though he called her FW for "Future Wife," he was too focused on himself and his work to have a romantic relationship. Syd wanted more: she wanted to be the center of a man's world someday, after she'd gone on her travels.

Although Nathaniel was a complex man, they'd developed a friendship and she'd grown to understand him. Nathaniel was motivated by a need to be as important as his hero brother.

Who still hovered over her desk.

"Let me call his supervisor, Alan Gustafson," she offered. "Maybe he knows when Nathaniel will be back."

She rang Alan.

"Mr. Gustafson? Nathaniel Keen's brother is here at the reception desk asking to see—"

"I'll be right down."

CLICK.

Odd. Alan rarely left his office for anything but liquid lunches.

"He's coming down to speak with you," she said.

"You think my brother's disappearing act is normal?"

"If they gave him a challenging project, he might isolate himself to get it done."

"Sounds like you know him better than I do."

"I see him more."

"Guilt trip. Ouch."

She eyed him. "Interesting that you'd go there. I didn't."

His gaze drifted to the pen jar on the desk. He might be a military tough-guy, but she read regret in those amazing turquoise eyes. Good, he should feel regret.

Family came first in her book, before friends or dreams, or military medals. Dalton Keen left home for the military and never looked back, leaving his little brother to defend himself against peers who belittled the brilliant boy. It didn't surprise Syd that Nathaniel's social skills were stunted.

From this short interaction with his big brother, she figured Nathaniel could have learned a lot from hanging around Dalton, the charmer.

"Sydney, is this Mr. Keen?" Alan said coming around the corner.

"Sydney?" Dalton raised a brow, eyeing the nameplate that read *Angela*.

"I'm filling in." She smirked.

She didn't like being caught in a lie, but instinct told her the less this man knew about her the better. Especially after she'd found out he was Nathaniel's brother, the secret agent.

The men shook hands. "Alan Gustafson. I'm your brother's supervisor. What can I do for you?"

"I haven't heard from Nate in over a week."

"Yes, well." Alan glanced at Syd, then back to Dalton. "We all know how Nathaniel gets when he's absorbed in a project."

"No, I'm afraid I don't. Anything you can tell me would help ease my fear that something's happened to him."

"Happened? As in foul play?"

"Yes, sir."

"Not to worry, Mr. Keen. Your brother is fine. I received a call from him this morning."

"Really? That's a relief. Where is he?"

"We sent him on assignment overseas. He's not due back for another ten days."

Chapter Two

Nate left the country and didn't tell Dalton? Not likely. They might not have the best relationship, but the kid would have told Dalton if an overseas trip was on the agenda.

"I'm surprised he hasn't returned my calls, just to let me know he's okay," Dalton pushed.

"I'm sure he meant to but he's buried in this project. It's security work, for the government," he said, as if that should satisfy Dalton.

It didn't. He glanced at the girl and noticed a questioning look on her face. It seemed that Angela, or Sydney, or whatever she called herself today, was as surprised as Dalton to hear that Nate had been sent across the world.

"When you speak with him again, could you ask him to call me? We need to discuss some family business."

Dalton shook the man's hand, pretending he was satisfied with the answer. Something felt off, but Dalton couldn't put his finger on it. Then again, maybe his agent training was making him paranoid.

Alan disappeared down the hall and Dalton turned to the girl who nibbled at her lower lip.

"What?" he asked.

"Hmm?" She snapped her attention from her papers and

pinned him with striking violet eyes, eyes that radiated way too much innocence for Dalton's taste.

"What's going on in that cute blond head of yours?" he asked.

"I need to eat lunch."

"I'll buy."

He needed someone on the inside. She knew Nate. She was perfect.

"No, thanks. I brought lunch."

She waved her lunch bag. "Besides, I have to wait for Angela to get back.

"I can wait."

"You really shouldn't," she said, apprehension in her voice.

Why? What had Nate told her about him? Nah, Dalton was dreaming up a conspiracy where there was none.

"Another time, perhaps?" Dalton said.

"Sure, when your brother gets back we can all go out for a bite to eat."

She studied the calendar tablet on the desk as if it held the answer to world peace.

"Right, well, thanks for your help." He paused. "Sydney."

"You're very welcome, Mr. Keen." She didn't look up.

He took his cue to leave, went outside into the beautiful Seattle sunshine and cursed himself for coming all the way over here for nothing. He didn't get to see his brother and didn't get much satisfaction from the boss's explanation.

Even if Nate was on assignment he could have called Dalton back, unless Nate was ticked off that Dalton had ignored Nate's conspiracy theories. Hell, the kid was a computer dork, not a government agent.

Dalton pulled out his cell and tried another tact. He called Nate and it went into voice mail again.

"Hey, bro," Dalton started. "Look, I'm sorry if I was rude when you called. I blew it, okay? I need your help again, buddy. Could you give me a call? Thanks."

He hung up and walked to his truck. If Nate was intentionally ignoring Dalton's calls, this would snap him out of it. A call for help from his older brother would be too tempting to pass up. Damn, Dalton wanted to hear that his brother was okay.

Since when did Dalton become the protective big brother? He hadn't given the kid much thought growing up. But ever since Dalton hit thirty he'd started questioning things, including his relationship with Nate. Was it his new protector role he'd taken on as an NSA agent? Now at thirty-three, hostage rescue was his specialty. Maybe that need to save and protect innocents had spilled over into his personal life.

Whatever the reason, he needed closure before he shipped out on his next assignment.

He got in his truck and leaned against the headrest. Eyeing Locke headquarters, he hoped Sydney would use the front entrance to leave for lunch. If not, he'd wait until the end of the day and follow her home. Creepy, but necessary if he was going to figure out if his brother was truly on assignment, or if something else was going on.

From the expression on the girl's face, he suspected it was door number two.

"What have you gotten yourself into, little brother?"

SYDNEY THOUGHT IT ODD that Alan said he'd sent Nathaniel overseas when she knew he didn't have an updated passport. They'd discussed it a few weeks ago when he'd caught her going through travel brochures and admitted he'd had the chance to visit Paris last month, but didn't have a current passport.

She'd added it to her To Do list since one of her responsibilities as IT Admin was to keep the guys organized.

Another job was to make their travel arrangements, and she'd made none for Nathaniel.

She found a spot at the lakefront in downtown Kirkland and nibbled her hummus and tomato sandwich. The Nathaniel mystery niggled at her brain. He wasn't organized enough to make his own travel arrangements, and he didn't have a passport. How did Locke, Inc. manage to send Nathaniel overseas? She shuddered at the thought of Nathaniel trying to navigate his way through a foreign country without the benefit of a Syd-approved itinerary.

She put down her sandwich to text him. Surely he'd answer her. He might be angry with his brother, but Nathaniel and Syd were tight.

Hey, X! Where R U?

She hit Send. Picking up her sandwich, she considered the overseas Locke offices that specialized in government-related projects.

"Looks good."

She jumped, startled by the sound of Dalton's voice. He sat on the bench beside her and eyed the sandwich. "Got an extra?"

"You followed me?"

"Too creepy?"

"Uh, yeah." She scooted a few inches away.

"Sorry, but I sense you care about my brother so I thought maybe you could help me."

"I know as much as you do." She took a bite of her sandwich.

"No, actually, that's not true."

"Excuse me?" He was right. Not only did she know his brother better than Dalton, but she also knew the implausibility of Nathaniel hopping a plane to another country without Syd's knowledge.

Dalton stretched his arm across the back of the park bench.

Too close. Every time he came within five feet of her, her body warmed with attraction.

"What did my brother tell you about me?" he asked.

"Not much, why?"

"He had to tell you something that makes you cringe every time you see me."

"I was looking forward to a peaceful lunch, that's all."

He eyed a group of children chasing ducks into the lake. "It is peaceful here. I can see why you like it."

Then he aimed his blue-green eyes at her. She wished he'd put his sunglasses back on.

"I sense you like my brother," he said.

"As a friend," she clarified.

"And I love him, as a brother."

"Really? You have a funny way of showing it."

"Ah, he did talk about me. You heard all about how I abandoned him and left him at the mercy of our drunk father."

That threw her. Maybe she didn't know Nathaniel as well as she thought she did.

"No, actually, he never said anything like that."

"What did he say?"

She studied him, wondering what caused this man to leave his family behind to pursue danger.

"Nathaniel said you're a hero and he'd do anything to be more like you."

"I sense you have a problem with that?"

"Sure. In the words of the great Ralph Waldo Emerson, 'envy is ignorance…imitation is suicide.'"

"Deep. What does it mean?"

"It means we need to accept ourselves for who we are instead of trying to become someone else."

"And you've done this? Learned to accept yourself?"

"I'd like to think so."

"Congratulations."

"You're making fun of me." She wrapped up her sandwich.

"No, wait."

He touched her arm and she glared at his fingers. Strong, male fingers that warmed her skin.

"I'm being a jerk," he said. "But I'm worried about him. I've been a deadbeat brother, I know that," he started. "I'm trying to make it up to Nate, but it's not easy. We're completely different. I thought you could help me understand him."

With a sigh, she leaned against the bench and gazed across the lake. "What do you want to know?"

"Does he do this a lot? Disappear?"

"Only one other time that I can remember, about a year ago. We'd made plans to go to Bumbershoot, but he blew me off. He was AWOL for a week. When he showed up, he was very apologetic about standing me up, which was typical."

"What do you mean?"

"The genius types get so wrapped up in projects that they forget about time, or place, or even people. It can be hurtful, but there's something about your brother I find endearing. He's sweet and caring, so I accept him for who he is."

"You're more forgiving than most women I know."

"Life's too short to hold on to resentment."

"What about work projects? Has he been sent out of town for weeks at a time before?"

"Yes, but not overseas." She sighed. "That's the odd thing. He's part of the U.S. group, not International. There's no reason for them to send him overseas. Besides, I don't think he has a passport."

"Everyone's got a passport."

"Not your brother. His expired and we were in the process of getting him a new one."

"When did you speak with him last?"

"Over a week ago."

"How did he sound?"

"Like Nathaniel: scattered, but excited about the premier of the new *X-Men* movie. We're supposed to go together but he never called to confirm." She squared off at him. "I always made him confirm to be sure we were really going out."

"But you aren't dating?"

"We're friends."

"Does he see it that way?"

"Yes, although he calls me FW for 'Future Wife.'"

"Really?"

"It's a joke. I've been very clear that I'm not interested in a relationship."

"Why not?"

"Now you're getting personal."

"What, you've been burned?"

"You don't stop, do you?"

He winked. And she fought the urge to kiss him.

Yikes, maybe she needed a relationship after all, even if it was just for casual sex.

"Why no boyfriend?" Dalton pushed.

"I have plans to travel."

"Men can travel."

"Being committed to another person complicates things. I want my freedom to see the world. End of conversation."

"Wait, back to my brother. Even though he's an absent-minded goofball—"

"Genius," she corrected.

"That, too. Even a scatterbrain would let someone know he was leaving the country, right?"

"Not necessarily. He doesn't have a lot of friends."

"But he'd tell you, right?"

"Probably."

"Be honest, you sense something is off here, too, don't you?"

"I guess."

"Good, then help me figure out what it is. Be my spy at Locke."

She packed up her lunch and stood. "I can't do anything to risk my job, sorry."

"You wouldn't be risking anything. Listen for me, notice things. Better yet, you have access to his office?"

"Yes," she answered, walking to her car. He followed. Again, too close.

"Go through his desk and look for signs that he was planning to leave the country. Ask his coworkers. You're his friend. They won't suspect anything."

She unlocked the door to her ten-year-old Honda and felt his hand on her shoulder. She turned to him. That intense look in his eyes softened.

"I wouldn't normally be pushy, but…it's our mom. She needs us right now."

She couldn't imagine not being there for her mother when she'd grown ill. Her resolve started to crumble. Nathaniel had been kind to her, saved her job, shared his DVDs and chocolates when she needed an afternoon boost.

"Give me your number," she said.

He pulled a card from his wallet and handed it to her.

"I'll call if I find anything," she said.

"Want to give me your number?"

"No." She shot him a smile, got in her car and drove off, ignoring the handsome man who loomed in the rearview mirror. He was probably stunned that she'd denied him her phone number.

She couldn't help it. The man scared her in ways she

couldn't articulate. On some level she was still a small town girl, inexperienced and trusting. Dalton Keen was the type of man a girl like Syd could fall for against her better judgment.

Yet she had decided years ago that she wouldn't get involved until after she'd traveled, and even then it would be with a nice, gentle man, someone who would put her first. That was the one thing about her parents' relationship she'd always admired: Skip and Leanne Trent adored each other. Syd expected nothing less from her future partner.

As friends went, she was worried about Nathaniel. Dalton was right on when he called him naive and trusting. It was Nathaniel's brilliance that sometimes blinded him to what stared him in the face. That's why anyone who got close to Nathaniel felt the need to protect the pretty-boy genius. Yet not many people got close.

She drove back to Locke headquarters and breezed through the front door.

"Psst, Sydney?" Angela said.

Syd stopped at the reception desk.

"I hear a very handsome guy was here looking for Mr. Keen."

"Word travels like hot lava around here."

"Who was he?"

"Nathaniel's brother."

"Handsome, huh?"

"I guess. If you like the bruiser types."

"I do, I do."

Sydney glanced at the girl's desk, an utter mess in only an hour. "Hey, give me those messages for Nathaniel," Syd said. "Someone should be responding to them."

Dropping off messages would give her the perfect excuse to get into Nathaniel's office and check things out. Maybe if she eased Dalton's fears, he'd go away.

"Did you give him your number?" Angela asked, handing her the messages.

"Who?"

"The handsome brother."

"Nope."

"Why not?" Angela inquired in an incredulous tone.

"Not my type."

"Give him my number." She leaned forward and grinned.

"I doubt I'll be seeing him again but if I do, I'll tell him to call the switchboard." Syd took the elevator to the Technology floor on seven and shoved her purse in her desk drawer.

"Sydney?" Drew Crane approached her desk. "Can you work on this PowerPoint presentation for me?"

"Sure. Hey, have you seen or heard from Nathaniel recently?"

"No. Figured he was on assignment. Why do you ask?"

She shrugged, trying to play it cool. "He's got some DVDs of mine I'd like to get back. When do you need the PowerPoint?"

"By the end of the day. I started it, so you shouldn't have too much to do."

Which in Drew language meant it was a mess.

"Okay, no problem."

She glanced down the hall at Nathaniel's dark office. It had been dark for a week. She got up to deliver his messages when another computer tech came by with a request to check on an order he'd placed for a headset. The afternoon flew by with Syd focused on getting her work done as more requests landed on her desk.

Finally around four, when most of the guys had left early for the weekend, Syd ambled toward Nathaniel's office and entered the doorway. It was too neat, as if someone had gone through his things and straightened up to make it look like they hadn't. Now she was being paranoid. But she was the only one Nathaniel let organize his things, primarily because she didn't judge him for having superhero Pez dispensers or comic books in his bottom drawer.

She didn't tease him. She appreciated him. And okay, maybe she missed him. She decided to text him again.

Where are you? I need my *X-Men* DVD back!

She hit Send.

And heard a beep.

She placed the stack of urgent messages on the desk and opened the top drawer, then the next one in search of the source of the beeping. And there, in the bottom drawer, was Nathaniel's PDA beeping an alert that he had a message. Odd. Nathaniel never went anywhere without his BlackBerry.

"What are you doing in here?" Alan accused from the doorway.

"Organizing as usual." She shut the drawer and shot him a bright smile. "These guys are all slobs. Hey, I noticed these urgent messages on his desk," she lied, grabbing them. "You want them? I'd hate for something to fall through the cracks. Since you sent Nathaniel overseas, I figured he won't be answering them."

She sauntered to the door and handed them to Alan. He snatched them from her hand. "You shouldn't be in here when he's gone."

"Oh, sorry. He usually asks me to tidy things up when he's out to give him a sense of order when he returns. You know Nathaniel, chaos is his middle name." She chuckled and walked toward her desk. Something was definitely wrong. Nathaniel would never leave without his PDA, fondly named Parker, after Peter Parker.

Alan followed her, a little too closely, making her skin crawl.

"When do you think he's coming back?" she casually inquired as she sat behind her desk.

Alan towered over her. "Why are you asking so many questions?"

So many? She'd asked one. She'd asked when Nathaniel was coming back. She sensed Alan had been drinking, only this time he wasn't the friendly drunk, he was the obnoxious jerk.

"He's got my *X-Men* DVD and I need it back," she explained. "He's not returning my calls."

"*X-Men* DVD?"

"Yeah, the next movie is opening this weekend and I'd like to watch the previous one to get psyched about the new one." She shuffled papers on her desk. "The jerk has had it for two months."

She opened the PowerPoint file and hit Print. "Gotta get this to Drew before five." She stood, but Alan didn't budge.

The hair on the back of her neck bristled. She sensed an oncoming sleazy harassment moment. She'd successfully avoided them up to this point, not wanting to jeopardize her job by lodging a complaint.

He didn't touch her. Instead, he smiled. "You've been doing a super job for our team these past few months."

"Thanks." A super job? Uh-oh, here comes the other shoe, more like a size twelve boot, right between the eyes.

"I plan to express my appreciation in your upcoming review," he added.

"Double thanks."

"You're welcome." He started back toward his office, hesitated and turned to her. "Although, I'd hate to have to temper my enthusiasm due to your unprofessional behavior."

"I'm sorry, I don't understand."

"Yes, I think you do. Stay focused on the job, Sydney, not the people. Enjoy your weekend."

And with that cryptic and threatening comment, he went back into his office and shut the door.

She deflated in her chair. Okay, she didn't need to be hit over the head with a frying pan. Alan made it clear if she didn't stop singing her "Where is Nathaniel?" tune she would be punished in her review, which meant losing her perk of a month's paid leave, the one thing that had kept her going in this mundane job.

She'd call Dalton, tell him about the PDA and resign as his spy. The veiled threat from Alan was too creepy to ignore. Besides, for all she knew, Nathaniel left Parker behind because he was in a hurry to make his flight.

Not likely.

"Doesn't matter. You're done taking care of the world, remember?" she reminded herself out loud.

It was time for Syd to think about her own priorities for a change. Besides, Nathaniel was a grown man. As she'd said to his brother, Nathaniel could take care of himself.

NATE BROUGHT HIS KNEES to his chest and tried to stop his body from shivering. They'd stripped him of everything but his boxers and told him to get comfortable.

In a ten-foot-long cell that felt like an icebox.

He'd given them what they'd wanted, the primary password to his laptop. They had access to his files.

But not all of them. They'd never find the master labyrinth file, hidden in a secret chamber that only Nate could access. He'd die before he'd give that up.

Please God, help me be brave enough to die.

The door creaked open and adrenaline pulsed through Nate's blood. He didn't look up.

"And how are we this morning, Mr. Keen?" the familiar voice asked.

Nate didn't answer. He struggled to stop his body from shivering.

"I'm wondering, have you told us everything we need to know about your laptop?" the man asked.

"Yes."

"And no one else knows about your discovery?"

"No."

"Look at me when you speak."

Nate glanced at the short, bald man who'd questioned him last night. Standing beside him was a giant with meat mallets for fists.

"No one knows Locke designed the microchip." Although he'd tried to tell Dalton, who was too busy to listen.

The bald man leaned against the wall and smiled. "Let's make sure, shall we?" He nodded to the bruiser hovering in the doorway. A sinister smile curled the giant's lips.

Nate squeezed his eyes shut.

Dalton, help me.

Chapter Three

Dalton needed to get back to Port Townsend and pack. *Be ready*, his C.O. had said.

He'd be a lot more ready if he could resolve this thing with his brother. Dalton felt bad about involving the girl but he needed to track down Nate and make sure he was okay. He sensed the girl would fall for a hardship story like a needy parent. That's what Dalton was trained to do: manipulate.

"Kid, where are you?" He eyed Nate's condo from across the street. Maybe the girl was right: Nate was a big boy. He could take care of himself.

Yeah, you keep rationalizing, Keen, and maybe the guilt will dissolve. Guilt for abandoning his brother when he needed him most. But Dalton had a life to live, a life far away from Sterling, Illinois.

And what about Nate's life? a voice taunted, the voice that occasionally reminded Dalton what life must have been like for Nate and Mom after he'd left.

The old man was a terrorizing bastard when he'd been drinking. Maybe he didn't hit his loved ones, but he beat them up emotionally, which was his way of feeling better about himself.

Dalton figured Mom took the abuse because she didn't

want her boys to grow up in a broken home. Had she really done them any favors? After all, Dalton had no interest in finding a good woman and settling down. A happy marriage was an oxymoron, pure fantasy created by greeting card companies.

Keen family members coped in their own way: Dalton joined the army at eighteen, Mom lived in a world of denial, peach pies and ladies club meetings, and Nate buried himself in books, absorbing more knowledge than any normal person should have.

The kid got a full ride to college, earned his bachelor's and master's degrees, and graduated with multiple job offers in hand.

He'd even been lucky enough to meet Cute Sydney with the violet eyes, the very type of girl his brother should date. She was genuine, adorable and smart, a triple whammy.

Dalton would be jealous if he were in the market for a girl, which he wasn't. Females drove him nuts with their head games. Nope, Dalton enjoyed his uncomplicated life minus females, although he enjoyed one in his bed now and then.

"What's with all the thinking?" Dalton said to himself, getting out of his car and heading toward Nate's Kirkland condo.

A woman in tight, red running shorts breezed out of the building. Dalton grabbed the door and nodded at her, but she was absorbed in whatever was playing on her iPod.

"Not bad, little brother," Dalton muttered, figuring if other tenants looked anything like Ms. Tight-running-shorts, Nate wouldn't have to go far to get a date.

Not that dating seemed like a priority. Even his relationship with Cute Syd was one of friendship, not romance, at least from her perspective. Did Nate feel the same way? Hell, Dalton wouldn't know.

He hesitated outside his brother's unit and glanced down

the hall to make sure no one was around. He picked the lock and let himself inside. The door clicked shut and he automatically drew his gun at the sight of the trashed apartment. Newspapers, magazines and books littered the floor; furniture cushions were out of place.

Calming the adrenaline rush with a slow, deep breath, he listened to determine if the intruders were still in the condo.

He made his way down the hall to Nate's bedroom, which had also been tossed. He finished his search of the condo. He was alone. He returned his gun to its holster.

A picture frame lay haphazardly on the floor next to the dresser. He picked it up and was staring at a photo of Dalton in dress uniform.

"Damn hero worship."

He placed it next to a photograph on the dresser of Nate and Cute Syd posing by the brass pig at Pike Place Market. Someone, probably the girl, had added bubble thoughts to the picture. Hers read:

I can't believe I forgave the Space Cadet.

Nate's read:

I promise to be a better friend.

Interesting.

Dalton had no idea if anything was missing. He searched the second bedroom and noticed the computer in the corner. Surely a thief would have taken the electronics.

The slam of the front door echoed down the hall. He slipped his gun from its holster and edged toward the living room. It sounded like his visitor was opening cabinets and kitchen drawers in search of something.

Dalton spun around the corner. "Freeze!"

"Ah!" Sydney tossed a glass in the air, slipped and fell on her butt.

Oops.

He holstered the Glock and went to the kitchen. She sat with her eyes closed, gripping her white sweater in front with both hands.

"Uh, sorry about that," he said.

"You should be," she countered. "I could have had a stroke."

"You're too young to have a stroke."

"I wouldn't be so sure."

She was breathing heavy and it was turning him on.

"Here." He stepped over the shattered glass and extended his hand.

"Don't touch me." She batted it away.

"I don't want you to cut yourself on the sharp edges getting up. Come on."

She narrowed her eyes and took his hand. Her skin felt just as he'd guessed it would, soft and fragile, and when he pulled her up she stumbled into him, teasing his senses with a familiar scent, like the lily of the valley flowers growing wild outside his family home.

"You can let go of me now," she snapped.

"Right, sorry."

"Jerk."

"I said I was sorry."

"You pointed a gun at me!" she protested, making her way into the living room.

"I carry a firearm for work."

"Well, ducky for you."

She righted the cushions on the sofa and collapsed, tipping her head back, closing her eyes.

He'd scared the crap out of her. It wouldn't take much. This adorable girl lived a safe, gentle life in such contrast to Dalton's violent one.

"Can I get you something to drink?" he offered.

"A shot and a beer." She opened one eye. "I'm kidding."

"I figured."

A few seconds passed. "I was debating on calling the police," he said.

"Why?" She cocked her head to the side and eyed him.

He motioned toward the messed up condo. "Someone broke in."

She burst out laughing. Okay, she was manic.

"What?" he asked.

"This?" She caught her breath, leaned forward and scooped peanuts littering the coffee table into a bowl. "This is normal."

"Oh." He felt like a jerk. He didn't even know his brother was a Class A slob. "I thought the place had been tossed."

She picked up a few magazines and old newspapers, still giggling to herself.

"Why are you here, and how did you get in?" he asked, irritated by the fact she knew more about his brother than he did.

"I've got a key."

"Really?" He raised a brow.

"You would go there." She stood and continued plucking things from the floor.

"Go where?"

"To the sex thing. It's always about the sex with men."

"And *that's* a bad thing?"

She shook her head with disapproval.

"Why did he give you a key, then?"

"I water his plants twice a week on my way home."

"And you're not his girlfriend?"

"Nope."

He must have looked confused.

"I take care of people," she said. "It's what I do."

"But you weren't concerned when you didn't see him for a week?"

"He doesn't check in with me. I told you, when he gets lost in projects I don't hear from him for a while."

"This could be one of those times?" he asked, hopeful. He needed the assurance so he could head out on his next assignment guilt-free.

"Could be," she said. "Only…"

"What?" He leaned against the wall and studied her.

She slapped a pile of newspapers and magazines to the kitchen counter. "He left Parker, his PDA at work, which is odd. I mean, if he was in a hurry and forgot it, wouldn't it be sitting on his messy desk, or lying on the floor or something?"

"Where was it?"

"In his bottom drawer, the one reserved for candy and comic books."

"You're kidding."

"You really don't know him very well, do you?"

"We didn't talk much until recently."

It was convenient since Dalton was stationed so close. Stationed? Is that what you called his time off to recuperate from a botched mission?

"Since you know him better than I do, tell me if I should be concerned about the disappearing act," he said.

"I'd normally say no, but a few things are bothering me. The PDA for one, then my boss's subtle threat." She grabbed a glass from the cabinet and filled it with water. "He caught me in your brother's office and seemed more peeved than usual. Even made a veiled threat that I'd better keep my relationships professional or else."

"Or else what?"

"He'd mark me down on my review."

"That's absurd."

"And weird that he's making this threat now. Nathaniel and I have been friends for a few years, but now suddenly I'm supposed to stay away from him?"

She motioned to another glass and Dalton nodded that he could use some water.

More like tequila.

She filled the glass and handed it to him, then reached into the closet for a broom to sweep up the broken glass. "I guess it's a good thing I ran into you, even if you scared the pants off me."

Interesting choice of words.

"I have to turn in my resignation," she said.

"They're forcing you to resign because you were caught spying on my brother?" he asked.

"No, I'm not resigning at Locke. I'm resigning as your spy. I can't risk a bad review."

"But Nate's your friend."

"And he understands that I'm in this job primarily for the month's paid leave I get after three years of service. That's only six months away."

"Why's the leave so important to you?"

She emptied the dustpan of broken glass into the metal waste can. "All I've ever wanted to do was travel, see Europe, Greece, South Africa. I can make that happen through my job at Locke."

So the girl had her goal and Dalton had his: moving on to his next assignment. Where did that leave Nate?

"Can I ask one more favor?"

"You can ask." She sipped her water.

"Can you go through the apartment with me and see if anything's missing?"

"Okay, but that's it. After that, I'm done."

AS THEY WENT THROUGH Nathaniel's things, Syd noticed Dalton's expression change from curiosity to surprise when he found a collection of military books on his brother's shelves.

"Why's he reading these?" Dalton asked.

"Why do you think?" She opened the freezer and pulled out the special bag of string beans.

"Do not tell me he was going to enlist." He eyed her as she dug into the frozen vegetables. "Hungry?"

"He keeps his secret key in the freezer." She pulled out the silver key. "Voilà. Follow me." She led him into Nathaniel's home office. "As to why he was reading military books, I'm guessing it was his way of feeling connected to you."

"All he had to do was call."

"Uh-huh." She opened the folding closet doors and tossed blankets and clothes aside. "There's a hidden compartment in his closet floor."

"For what?"

"He keeps Niko down there."

"Who?"

"His top secret laptop he named after the famous scientist Nikola Tesla."

She stuck the key in the lock and opened the trap door, but it was empty. "Weird, he always keeps it here."

"Maybe he needed it for his work project?"

"Maybe."

But something felt off. Nathaniel was paranoid about taking Niko out of his apartment, for any reason. If he needed something from the laptop, he'd either e-mail it to himself or transfer it onto a jump drive.

"What?" Dalton asked.

She stood up and realized he was too darn close. She

brushed past him into the living room and knelt beside Nathaniel's DVD cabinet to organize his movies.

"What's bothering you?" Dalton pressed as he followed her.

"Nathaniel's my friend. I'm worried about him."

"He's lucky to have friends like you."

She plucked her *X-Men* DVD from the floor. "There aren't many of us."

"Why?" Dalton grabbed a handful of computer magazines and stacked them on the glass coffee table.

With a sigh, she righted the last of the DVDs. "He doesn't have the best social skills. He's uneasy around people."

"But comfortable around you?"

"Don't read anything into it. He does well with one-on-one relationships. But he's picky about that one."

"So, there's no one else besides you?"

"I've seen him go out with a couple of guys at work, Drew Crane and Pete Desai. Last week I saw Nathaniel talking to a new girl on the team, Laura something. I don't know her last name."

"I'll need their contact information," he said.

"Good luck with that."

"Can't you get it for me?"

She squared off at him. "Look, chief, I said I'd help go through the condo and see if anything was missing. I won't breach company policy and give you personal information about Locke employees."

"No one will know where I got it."

"Aren't you a secret agent? Can't you get it through work?"

"They frown on us using government information systems for personal matters."

"Then track them down the same way you found me. I'll tell you when they take lunch and you can stalk them."

"Ah, I have a feeling my charm won't be as effective on men."

"Oh, so I'm a pushover?"

"Nah, you're sweet."

Syd was tired of being sweet. She'd been sweet her whole life. Sweet Syd, the girl who was always bright and happy. Sweet Syd, the devoted daughter who nursed two parents through cancer.

Sweet Syd, who desperately wanted to travel and see the world, yet working with this man was threatening her chance for that very adventure.

"What did I say?" Dalton asked, studying her.

"I've got to go." She shoved the *X-Men* DVD into her purse.

"Wait, Sydney." But she was determined to get away from Dalton Keen's charm, to shelve her concern for a friend who very likely didn't think to tell people who cared about him where he was going and when he'd be back. All this worry was probably for nothing.

"What did I do?" Dalton asked.

She hesitated in the doorway. Okay, she was being rude. She turned to him. "You didn't do anything it's just—"

Her vibrating cell distracted her. She dug into her purse, pulled out her phone and retrieved a text message. It was from a number she didn't recognize:

on assignment. be back in two weeks. don't let Pete swipe my Enforcer comic books. thanks, nate

"Here." She handed Dalton the phone. The text should make them both feel better.

It didn't. Nathaniel always signed off as *X*, for Professor Xavier from *X-Men*. She was being paranoid. Nate was probably stressed out about his current assignment.

Yet if someone else had sent it, he or she was going to a lot of trouble to make it look like Nathaniel was okay.

Which meant he was most definitely not okay.

Dalton read the text and handed her the phone. "You said he left his PDA at work."

"They probably gave him another one."

He narrowed his eyes as if he sensed her concern.

"I need to go," she said. "I've got your number if anything comes up."

Syd marched down the hall to the elevator, anxious to get away from Nathaniel's apartment and his sexy big brother. She wasn't a coward, although a part of her felt like one for turning her back on Nathaniel. But she'd seen both parents through cancer and her older sister through an ugly divorce. Syd was tough, damn it, and didn't scare off easily.

She wasn't running from this situation as much as she was finally putting herself first. She'd spent the better part of her life taking care of everyone else. She didn't want anything to happen to Nathaniel, but his own family could follow up.

For once she'd let someone else do the caretaking, and she'd focus on herself. Who better to help the scatterbrained genius than his war hero brother?

DALTON CONTINUED GOING through Nate's things, looking for some kind of clue as to where his brother had gone. Dalton would have given up and gone back to Port Townsend if he hadn't recognized panic in the girl's eyes, panic hidden behind her carefree expression. She knew Nate better than anyone and was worried about him but wasn't in a place to do anything about it. Locke, Inc. had her by the golden handcuffs.

Going through the desk in Nate's home office, Dalton

stretched out his neck at the thought of using a set of hand-cuffs on the cute blonde as foreplay.

"Keen, you need to get laid, buddy, and quick."

But not by a sweet thing like Sydney. She was a love-her-and-marry-her type, the kind you didn't touch unless you were ready to commit. She claimed she didn't want to get involved because she yearned to travel. But he knew once she got the travel bug out of her system, she'd want love, marriage, kids and a minivan. Dalton was too smart to be sucked into that nightmare.

He could see why Nate liked having her around. Mom hadn't nurtured her boy genius, for fear of setting off the old man. Yet nothing stopped the bastard from taking out his frustrations on his wife and sons. Once the old man got a taste of his bullying power, it was like a drug. He wanted more.

Afraid his teenage temper might get the better of him, Dalton had left home before he hauled off and slugged the guy. Hell, Dalton didn't want to be locked up for assault before he could earn a purple heart.

Nate should have earned a purple heart for the mental abuse he had suffered from their father. Still, he'd done pretty well for himself professionally.

Dalton kept telling himself that to ease the guilt. He wondered what kind of damage the kid had sustained and buried deep inside.

His cell vibrated and he grabbed it, hopeful. The caller ID read his mother's number and he hesitated before answering. He really didn't need to talk to her right now.

"Keen," he answered.

"Dalton, it's Mom. Am I disturbing you?"

Sure, he was disturbed that she hadn't defended her sons from the beast.

"No, ma'am."

"I'm calling about your brother."

Dalton squeezed the phone. "You've heard from him?"

"No, not since my birthday. He always calls."

Not like Dalton. Sure, Dalton knew the date, but didn't like calling, offering good wishes to a woman who should have protected her sons. Okay, so it was passive-aggressive, but he couldn't help himself. Deep down he was still that little boy who, no matter how well he did in football, was always a failure in his father's eyes. Only after Dalton had grown up did he recognize his father's motivation was borne out of his own insecurities.

"What's up?" Dalton said.

"We're going through the attic, getting the house ready to put on the market and we found a few boxes of Nathaniel's things, inventions of some kind. I thought Natty might want to go through them before Edward throws them out."

Edward, her new man-in-charge. Dalton had never met him, but he assumed the guy was a carbon copy of the old man who'd died four years ago sucking on a bottle of Scotch.

"Why call me?" Dalton asked. He sounded rude. Couldn't help himself.

"I've left Natty messages but he doesn't return my calls. He told me you were stationed in Seattle and you boys have been hanging out."

Hanging out? Is that what Nate thought they were doing?

"He hasn't been returning my calls either. I think he's gone overseas for a work project."

"Well...I don't know what to do with his things."

She obviously wanted to rid herself of the memory of her boys.

"Send it to my APO address. I'll make sure he gets it."

"Oh, okay. I thought maybe..."

"What, Mom?"

"I haven't seen either of you in so long and I thought you could come for a visit, go through things and—"

"Help you pack up?" Nice, he doesn't hear from her in months and she calls for manual labor.

"No, I didn't mean—"

"Gotta go, Mom. I'll tell Nate to call you."

He hit End, went to the living room sofa and turned on the television. One thing he didn't need right now was to deal with his past. As he flipped through channels, he thought he heard a knock at the door.

The girl would use her key, right? Maybe it was Ms. Tight-running-shorts. Dalton couldn't get that lucky. He turned off the television.

Waited.

Nothing.

Must have been a knock from the apartment next door.

He flipped the tube back on and distracted himself with a news program.

Suddenly two suits bounded into the condo, one pulling Sydney alongside him and the other aiming his firearm at Dalton. He stood and raised his hands. The girl looked like she was about to have her second stroke of the night.

"Nathaniel Keen?" the older guy asked.

"No, sir, I'm his brother, Dalton."

The agent, Dalton guessed FBI, looked at Syd who nodded in affirmation.

"Is Nathaniel here?"

"No, sir."

"Check it out," the lead agent ordered the second guy, then drew his weapon on Dalton.

"What's this about?" Dalton asked.

The lead agent ignored his question as the younger agent,

tall with a military cut, went through the condo. A minute later he returned to the living room. "It's clear."

The older agent holstered his weapon. "I'm going to have to ask the two of you to come with us."

Chapter Four

The girl didn't say a word as the federal agents drove them to an undisclosed location for questioning.

What have you gotten yourself into, little brother?

Nate was a sweet kid. Sweet, brilliant and trusting. He must have stepped into a load of trouble by accident.

Or had Dalton dragged him into trouble by involving him in the microchip case? Nah, that was resolved. Three chips were found, the sender of the chips apprehended overseas. That case was history.

Then he remembered his little brother's message about recognizing information imbedded on the microchip: *I've seen those numbers before.*

Dalton thought the kid was making stuff up to keep big brother close and in his life. Pathetic that Dalton had driven him to that for fear he'd lose his big brother again.

Dalton would make it up to him when Nate resurfaced. If he resurfaced. Dalton eyed the suits in the front seat. They wanted Nate and he still didn't have a clue why.

They pulled into an underground parking garage and got out. Again, without a word, the agents led Dalton and Sydney to the elevators.

"Ya know, I had a really fun weekend planned," Sydney blurted out.

Hearing distress in her voice, Dalton pressed the agents. "Why are we here, exactly?"

"We have some questions about your brother. With any luck, you'll only be here a few hours," said the older agent. He'd identified himself as Agent Aronson back at the condo.

The younger agent with the crew cut scanned the parking lot as if expecting someone to jump out from behind a parked car firing an Uzi submachine gun.

In more silence, they took the elevator to the seventeenth floor and were led to an inside office with no windows. Made sense. They wanted Dalton and Sydney to feel completely isolated with no sense of time or place.

To feel completely vulnerable.

He knew their tactics but Sydney was completely out of her element.

"Down here, Ms. Trent," the younger agent said.

"I'd prefer we stay together," Dalton said, stepping between Syd and the agent.

For a second he thought the agent would challenge him. Instead, he glanced at his superior. Agent Aronson nodded and the younger guy stepped aside.

Aronson had called in while at Nate's condo for Dalton's background. Dalton saw the guy's eyes flare with interest when told what Dalton did for a living. Aronson probably didn't want to see his young agent get taken down by Dalton over something as little as separating Dalton and Syd during interrogation.

"Sydney?" Dalton reached for her hand.

She hesitated at first, as if hedging her bets as to which was worse: being with Dalton or being alone with the federal officer.

She slipped her petite fingers into his palm and he closed his hand, gently. "Let's get this over with."

Aronson led them into the room. Dalton positioned Syd beside him at the table and the agents sat across from them.

"Ms. Trent, you work with Nathaniel Keen?" Aronson asked.

"Yes."

"What can you tell us about him?"

"Hang on," Dalton interrupted. "How about you tell us why we're here?"

"It's a matter of national security."

"You're kidding."

"There's nothing funny about this, you cocky sonofa—"

"Weiss," Aronson warned his young counterpart, then readdressed Dalton. "I can't get into details, but it's of vital importance that we find your brother."

"You know what I do, right? That I'm with the NSA and work on the terrorist task force?"

"Yes."

"Tell me what's going on and maybe I can help."

"We were hoping you and Ms. Trent already knew what was going on."

"I've been trying to reach Nate for over a week and he seems to have disappeared," Dalton said. "Sydney works with him and hasn't been able to contact him, either, although, she got a text from him tonight."

"What did it say?" Agent Weiss asked, leaning against the table.

Syd crossed her arms over her chest in a defensive posture. "That he was away on business. That he's fine."

"Let's see your phone." Weiss put out his hand.

"Easy, man," Dalton warned. "She's not an accomplice to anything illegal here."

"You sure about that?"

"Here." Sydney dug the cell phone out of her purse and slapped it into his palm. "I have nothing to hide."

"Glad to hear it." Weiss checked her text messages. "I've got it."

"See if you can have it traced," Aronson ordered.

Weiss left them alone with the senior agent.

"You answer a few questions and I'll answer your questions. Fair enough?" Aronson asked.

Dalton nodded.

"When was the last time you saw your brother?"

"About two weeks ago." Keep the answers short, to the point.

"What was your business with him?"

"No business. He's my brother." The microchip smuggling case was top secret, way above this guy's pay grade.

"How did he seem to you?"

"Excited about some project he was working on." Dalton didn't say it was his microchip project.

"He didn't seem nervous?"

"Where are you going with this?"

Aronson put up his finger as if to say it wasn't Dalton's turn to ask questions.

"Did he mention anything about his work at Locke, Inc.?" Aronson continued.

"No, sir, he did not."

Aronson faced Sydney. "And the last time you spoke with him?"

"Um, I guess that would be Friday, September 14."

"You know the exact date?"

"He stood me up. Again."

"Really?" Aronson marked something on his legal pad. "Did he say why?"

"He said he'd lost track of things. I think it might have something to do with this big project they gave him at work."

"What project?"

"I don't know the details. His boss came down and told Dalton that Nathaniel was sent overseas on assignment, but I thought that was weird since he doesn't have a passport and…"

Dalton placed his hand on her knee to stop her.

She glanced at him. "What?"

"Take a breath, it's okay."

She was rambling on, probably nervous about being interrogated. He was trying to stop her before she shared too much information with the Feds. Too much? What was Dalton afraid of? He wasn't sure, but instinct told him to play this one close if he was to protect his brother.

Damn, had Nate gotten himself into legal trouble?

"Ms. Trent," Aronson started, shooting Dalton a warning glare. "Nathaniel doesn't have a passport?"

"Not that I know of. We were in the process of getting him one."

"And he didn't give you any reason to miss your date?"

"It wasn't a date, really. We're not romantically involved."

"That's not what he told us."

"You've spoken with my brother? When?" Dalton asked.

"I'll address that in a minute. Ms. Trent, about your relationship with Mr. Keen."

She fidgeted in her chair. "What did Nate say about me?"

"That you were the one person he could trust with his life. He called you his 'Future Wife.'"

She studied her fingers, folded in her lap. "Oh, Nathaniel," she whispered, then looked at Dalton. "I did not lead him on. We're good friends." She glanced at the agent. "Friends. You know, we like the same movies, go to the same stores like Golden Age Collectibles store at the Market because they have movie scripts, comic books and posters." She glanced at Dalton. "I'm doing it again, aren't I, talking too much?"

"It's okay." As long as she talked about movie posters she was fine. He didn't want her slipping and telling the Feds that the kid's secret laptop was missing, or that her boss had threatened her because she'd been snooping in Nate's desk at work. Dalton didn't want Sydney dragged into this mess because she'd befriended Nate.

"Continue," Aronson said, probably hoping she'd say something incriminating so they could keep her for a while.

Dalton sensed their desperation to find Nate.

"That's it, really," Syd said. "We're friends, but he still stands me up. I'm used to it. That's typical of a brilliant mind."

"Before he disappeared, did you notice anything odd about his behavior?" Aronson continued. "Was he anxious or paranoid?"

"Not anxious, but excited, like Dalton said. Then again, he's excited most of the time. Like a little kid, especially when he's discovered a new toy."

"A new toy?" Aronson questioned.

"You know, like a code translator or new program language. He develops all kinds of security programs for companies all over the world. And I think for the government, too, right?"

Aronson didn't answer.

Uh-oh. Is that what this was about?

"My turn," Dalton said. "Why the interest in my brother's whereabouts?"

"He's been working with us on a special project and has gone AWOL."

Nate was working with the Feds and didn't tell Dalton?

"Then, a few days ago, we noticed a wire transfer into his checking account for a hundred thousand dollars. We suspect he's opted for money over loyalty to his country."

"That's bull," Dalton snapped.

"Why? Because he's the brother of a war hero?"

"Because my kid brother is not a traitor. Someone's setting him up. He'd be an easy mark."

Sydney nodded enthusiastically. "Nathaniel's a nice guy, brilliant, but not very street-smart. I could see him being tricked into doing something illegal."

Dalton closed his eyes. *Great, thanks, Syd.*

"That didn't sound right," she corrected. "What I meant was, if Nathaniel was involved in anything bad, I'm sure he didn't know what he'd gotten himself into."

She glanced at Dalton. "Okay, I'll really stop talking now."

Dalton eyed Agent Aronson. "What kind of work were you doing with my brother?"

"It's classified."

"Then we have nothing more to say." He took Sydney's hand and stood.

"Sit down," Aronson ordered.

"Or what? You're going to lock me up? You don't want to mess with me."

"No, I don't, but I could use your help. Your brother trusts you, maybe if you could get in touch with him—"

"I could hand him over to you so you can lock him up without cause? Nah, not interested."

"Please." He motioned to the chairs. Dalton and Syd sat back down. "I'm against the wall here," Aronson started. "I'd like to think you're right, that your brother is innocent. But look at the facts. He disappeared, a few days later a large sum of money was deposited into his account and a few days after that, Homeland Security's computer caught a virus. Maybe if we work together we can help him."

Work together? Dalton's goal would be to protect Nate and theirs would be to lock him up.

"Okay, what can we do?" Dalton said. He knew how to play both sides against each other. At least if he was pretending to work with the Feds, he'd keep their activities in his sights.

"Work with us to find your brother. We'll give him every consideration when he's brought in. You have my word."

Which meant nothing to Dalton. He knew better than to trust this suit that wanted to nail his brother for something he didn't do.

"I'll see what I can do," Dalton said.

"Not just you, Keen. We need Ms. Trent to agree to help us, as well."

SYD WAS FURIOUS. At least Dalton had asked for her help and then respected her wishes when she resigned. The federal agents pretended to be asking, but she knew an order when she heard one. They ordered her to help find Nathaniel by being their spy at the office, again, putting her job and her dream to travel in jeopardy.

Syd and Dalton were dropped off at Nathaniel's condo and she headed for her car. It was after eight and she hadn't eaten dinner. Hunger wasn't what had her all fired up. Once again, fate had taken hold of her life and ripped control from her hands, much like the cancer had controlled her life for years while she cared for her mom and dad.

"I thought I was free, got my chance to do something on my own terms, see the world," she muttered to herself. "But no. The Space Cadet disappears and everything is up for grabs. I can't believe he told them I was his Future Wife. Thanks, Nate, thanks a lot."

"Sydney?" Dalton stepped in front of her.

She looked up. "What?"

"You don't have to do anything for the Feds you're not comfortable doing."

"Easy for you to say, Mr. Secret-agent-I've-got-a-gun-so-no-one-messes-with-me. Out of my way." She walked around him.

"Let me buy you dinner," he offered.

"Are you kidding? No thanks. Get out of my way, out of my life." *Out of my dreams.* There, she admitted it. She was attracted to him which was complicating things.

"Why are you angry with me?" he asked. "I'm not the one asking you to spy. I let you off the hook, remember?"

"But I'm back on, aren't I?"

"Syd, honey, look at me."

"Honey?" She squared off at him. "You called me *honey?* And your brother calls me his Future Wife. What is it with you guys?"

"You're upset, I understand. I would be, too."

"But you're not. No, you do this kind of thing all the time. You're threatened at gunpoint. You give up your life for your secret missions." She fished in her bag for her keys. "I'm a small-town girl trying to see the world. Why are you people messing with that?"

"Stop." He placed his hand on her arm and she froze in search of her keys.

Every time he touched her it felt like someone had squirted warm oil on her skin and massaged ever so gently.

"Why do you have to touch me all the time?" she whispered.

He slid his hand off her arm. "I'm sorry. I instinctively want to protect you."

"Well, buster, I'm tougher than I look. I took hapkido," she said with a nod.

He smiled, his cheek dimpling.

"You're laughing at me," she said.

"No, I'm sorry, I'm not. You're cute when you're all worked up."

"I'm tired of being cute." She waved her hand. "Go away. Leave me alone so I can figure out how to save my job."

"Let me at least buy you dinner."

"I desperately want go home."

"I'll bring dinner to you. What do you have a taste for?"

"Carbs, lots of 'em."

"Any particular kind?"

"Chocolate, wine, bread. In that order."

"You got it. Give me your address and I'll meet you there in half an hour."

She rattled off her address and swung open her car door. Her bag slipped from her shoulder throwing her off balance. Dalton cupped her elbow for support. She glared at his hand.

"Sorry," he said, putting his hands up. "Forgot, no touching."

Oh, corn fritters, why was she so sensitive about him touching her? She was naturally a touchy-feely type person. Heck, she'd touched Nathaniel plenty of times to ground him and help him focus, or to straighten his collar, or brush long, errant bangs off his forehead.

She tossed her bag into the passenger seat and got in her Honda. Had she unintentionally led Nathaniel on, giving him signals that she was interested in being more than his movie buddy?

Dalton dipped his head. "See you soon. Drive safe."

He shut the door, shot her that charming smile and headed for his car.

Call him back! Tell him not to come over, not to bring sinful carbs or that sinful body to her place. Grr.

"I'm an insane person. Out of my mind," she said, pulling out onto Lake Washington Boulevard.

Sure she was. Her whole life had been tipped upside down and sideways thanks to Nathaniel's monkey business. And now she was stuck partnering with his big, sexy brother, Dalton, the charming warrior who tempted her with those blue-green eyes and made her fantasize about hot, sweaty sex.

Hot, sweaty sex? *Snap out of it!* She had to work with the federal agents to find Nathaniel so they'd leave her alone. Then Dalton would go away, it would all go away, and she could get back to business.

The business of traveling, exploring…living.

She sighed and pondered why she'd waited so long. She'd had enough money to take a small trip after her mom and dad had passed. She would have survived for a while without a job. Yet she chose to sock it away and find another means to make it happen. Mom and Dad waited to travel and got sick before they could enjoy the adventure.

And now Syd was against the wall, forced into servitude with hunky Dalton Keen. If the Feds weren't happy with her performance as their unofficial spy, what would they do? Accuse her of treason? She shuddered at the thought of being locked up.

"Don't think about it. Focus." The problem was she couldn't get Dalton's blue-green eyes out of her mind, eyes that radiated devastation when Agent Aronson had accused Nathaniel of being a traitor.

Dalton was tough, but Syd wasn't sure he could survive that kind of betrayal from his little brother.

"Nathaniel, please tell me you're too smart to be sucked into a mess like this."

She got home and slapped her purse onto the counter. Storm, her snow-white kitty, cowered beneath the Queen Anne chair.

"Hey, pretty kitty," she cooed, as she straightened the kitchen. Her favorite pink towel decorated with black cats was in the middle of the living room. "Storm, you bad girl. You've been playing mouse with the towels again?"

She snatched a towel from the floor and tossed it onto the kitchen counter.

Her eyes caught on the poster of Edinburgh Castle gracing her living room wall. What was she waiting for?

Pulling her hair back into a ponytail, she went to the computer in the breakfast nook to go online and check her savings account balance. She loved dreaming about the trip. It always brought her peace, especially when she'd had a particularly boring day or in this case a particularly unsettling one.

She signed on and typed in her password: *Rogue.*

A crash sounded from the bedroom. She eyed the empty spot beneath the chair. Fearing Storm would completely ruin her perfume bottle collection, Sydney raced down the hall to scold the cat.

"Storm! Stay away from my—"

She collided with a large man's chest. With a steely grip of her shoulders, he shoved her against the wall. The wind knocked from her lungs as she gasped for breath and fell to the floor. She pinched her eyes shut in shock. Why was this happening to her? She didn't have anything worth stealing.

Struggling to get her senses back, she felt him lean close. Damn it, all those hapkido classes and she was helpless?

"Your boyfriend sends his regards," he said against her ear with stale cigarette breath assaulting her nose.

The buzzer echoed from the living room.

"Until next time, lovely."

Chapter Five

Dalton punched the button for Syd's apartment a third time, but got no response. Was she blowing him off? Thought better of letting him come to her place for dinner?

A burly guy with slicked back salt-and-pepper hair wearing a smug expression swung the door open. Dalton took the opportunity to sneak inside, but glanced over his shoulder at the guy who got into a black sedan and peeled out of the lot.

Instinct made Dalton race up the stairs to the second floor. He found her apartment, dropped the groceries and banged on the door.

"Sydney? Open the door."

Nothing. Panic gutted him. The bruiser bastard had been here.

He picked the lock and went inside. "Sydney?"

Whimpering echoed from the hallway. He automatically pulled out his Glock and inched toward the source of the sound. As he turned the corner into the hallway, he froze at the sight of the trembling blonde huddled against the wall.

Control it. Focus. You can't help her if you lose your mind.

And he *was* losing it. He wanted to rush outside and track down the bastard who did this to her. The thought that he'd touched her…

"Are you alone?" he asked her.

"Y-y-y-yes."

He holstered his gun and knelt beside her, brushing the natural blond hair from her face. "What happened, sweetheart?"

She didn't scold him for the endearment.

"Big guy came out of my bedroom." She snapped her gaze to Dalton's and he wanted to pull her against his chest in comfort. "He said, he said…"

"Shh. Take a deep breath." He stroked her hair.

"I can't stop…shivering."

"It's the adrenaline. You'll be fine in a few minutes. Can you get up?"

She shook her head that she couldn't and hugged her knees to her chest. "Give me a minute."

Hell, he'd give her twenty. However long it took, Dalton would wait until she was ready to get up and talk about what happened.

"Permission to comfort you, Ms. Trent?" he asked, hoping to tease her out of her panicked state.

A very slight smile curled the corner of her lips. "Okay, just this once."

With an arm around her shoulders, he pulled her to his chest and rocked slightly. He'd never done this with a female before, but it felt natural to comfort her.

"It's okay now. You're safe."

She suddenly pushed away from him. "Nathaniel," she hushed.

"What about him?"

"That big guy, he said…he said my boyfriend sends his regards."

"You think he meant Nate?"

She started to get up. Dalton helped her, led her to the living room and gently guided her to sit on the sofa.

"I'll get you some water." As he found a glass, he considered the goon's comment. Dalton didn't believe Nate was involved with these bastards to betray his government, but the bruiser made it sound like he knew Nate. *Damn, Nate, are you unknowingly working with them to breach government security systems?*

It wouldn't surprise Dalton if his little brother was seduced by a clever manipulator.

He handed Sydney a glass of water. "Take a deep breath. That's it."

He knew what an adrenaline rush felt like. He'd depended on them for top performance in the field. But this girl, she shouldn't have had to experience the rush of fear and panic.

"Feeling better?" he asked.

"No."

"Want me to call a doctor?"

She shot him a look as if that were a ridiculous question. "I'm not that fragile."

"Sorry."

Fingering the rim of the glass, she glanced up with fear tinting her brilliant eyes. "The big guy said, 'until next time' like he was coming back."

He pulled her to his chest. "He won't hurt you. I promise."

Stroking her back, he closed his eyes and marveled at how comfortable this felt. Yes, he could see why his little brother adored this girl. She was sweet, yet tough.

"I'm sorry," she said, pushing away again.

He wished she'd stop doing that. "Don't be."

"I'm not used to strange men breaking into my apartment and threatening me."

"No, and you shouldn't be."

"How did you get in?"

"Special skills."

"Well, I'm glad you broke in to save me."

In Dalton's mind, he'd been too late.

"Did he indicate why he was here? What he wanted?" he pushed.

"No. I heard a crash from the bedroom and figured it was the cat, so I went to check it out. That's when he slammed me against the wall."

She pouted and rubbed the back of her head.

"Let me see." He touched a small lump on the back of her head. "I'll get you some ice."

"I'd rather have chocolate."

"I've got that, too. But first, do you want to call the police and report the break in?"

"Okay. No. I don't know. What good will it do? He's gone now."

Dalton should have detained the bastard to find out who he worked for and why he terrorized Sydney. Did they think she knew about Nate's business? After all Nate always referred to her as his Future Wife.

Syd hugged herself and glanced around her apartment. "I feel so gross. He touched my things."

Dalton wanted to put her at ease, tell her the guy wouldn't come back, that it was a one-time break-in.

Instinct told him otherwise.

"You'll feel better after you eat some chocolate." He started to get up but she didn't let go of his sleeve.

"Sorry." She released him.

"Sydney, look at me."

She glanced up, confusion flooding her eyes.

"You're okay," he said. "I'm here and I won't let anything happen to you."

She nodded. He got the groceries from the hallway and placed the bags on the counter. Sydney scanned the apartment, hugging herself tighter as if still feeling the intruder's presence. Dalton might be used to dealing with innocents' trauma, but he wasn't used to the feelings her vulnerability was stirring in his chest. Those emotions cut through to his heart, making him want to shield her from the ugliness.

The ugliness of his world. Another reminder of how different they were.

"Chocolate first, followed by wine?" he offered.

"Sure."

"What were you doing when you discovered the intruder?" He searched her drawers, found a corkscrew and went to work on the bottle.

"I was about to check my bank balances."

"Really?" He corked the wine.

"I like to dream about my trips. It makes me feel better when I'm having a bad day."

He poured two glasses of red wine and brought them to the sofa. Sitting beside her, he placed the glasses on the table. "We should probably wait a few minutes to let it breathe."

She cocked her head to the side. "You're teasing me, right?"

"What do you mean?"

"You know about wine?"

"Believe it or not, there's more to me than saving beautiful blondes and beating up bad guys." He smiled.

Her gaze drifted to his lips. Not good. A victim was known to do crazy things after an adrenaline rush, like kiss a man she shouldn't be kissing.

Dalton knew better. She was out of her mind, not thinking straight, and his little brother was probably in love with her. Dalton would not betray both Syd and his brother by doing anything dishonorable, however tempting.

"I've got the chocolate," he said, breaking the spell and

going into the kitchen. "I also bought a few frozen pot pies for real sustenance."

She sighed, as if she'd been holding her breath. "Good thinking, thanks. Need help with the oven?"

"No, ma'am. You go ahead and check your bank balance if that will cheer you up."

He put the pies on a cookie sheet and set the oven. Truth was, he had no intention of leaving her alone until this case was resolved. He puzzled over the intruder's comment about Nate sending his regards. Why would Nate send someone to hurt Sydney? He wouldn't. The guy was playing mind games with the girl.

And with Dalton. He didn't care what the Feds claimed. Dalton knew Nate would never do anything against the law or against Americans.

"Oh my God! No, that's completely wrong." Syd jumped to her feet and pointed at the computer screen.

"What's wrong?"

"It's all gone. They stole my money."

Dalton went to the computer and eyed the screen. Sure enough, her savings account balance read $19.75.

"That's impossible." She raced down the hall, scaring the cat, who jumped up and raced in the opposite direction.

"Where are you going?" he called after her.

"I have last month's statement in my hope chest."

"I'm sure it's a bank error," he lied. Hell, why did he get the feeling this, too, had something to do with his brother's indiscretions? Had the Feds swiped her nest egg to encourage her to cooperate?

Damn, he needed to know all the players in this. He pulled out his cell phone and called his buddy, Griffin Black. Although the guy was semiretired, he knew who could be trusted in AW-21 to help out with personal matters.

"Nicholas Drake," a man answered.

"Is this Nick Drake, formerly Griffin Black?"

"You in trouble again, Keen?"

Dalton appreciated the teasing tone.

"My little brother is missing and I need to figure out the players. I was wondering if you could recommend someone to help me out, someone discreet and trustworthy?"

"Ah, you mean like your friend Doc Winters?"

"Yeah, only not on the verge of a nervous breakdown."

Griff laughed. Dalton had never heard him laugh before. Civilian life with a loving woman definitely agreed with him.

"What about Zack Carter? You know him?" Griff offered.

"Uh, yeah, we've worked together."

Dalton was still unsure if Carter had figured out that Dalton defied orders to save the teenager at Pier 69. Even if he had, it appeared he'd kept his mouth shut.

"Carter's got top clearance and loves a good challenge." Griff paused. "I'm sorry to hear about your brother. You think it had something to do with his business, or yours?"

"Not sure yet. Could be related to the microchip case."

"Unfortunate."

"Yeah, well, thanks, buddy."

"You bet. Stay out of trouble. Don't make me have to come save your ass."

"Promise."

Dalton ended the call as Syd came into the room waving her bank statement. "See, look. $27,432.99. It's all there. But, but…" she stuttered, pointing at the screen.

He placed a calming hand to her back. "We'll go to the bank tomorrow and show them the statement. Everything will be fine."

She didn't take her eyes off the screen and Dalton stepped in front of her. "Syd?"

She aimed the bank statement at his chest. "They're not getting away with this, the bastards."

"That's the spirit."

"They think they can go into my account and steal my money, my parents' money? Two-thirds of that was money from their estate."

"And we'll get it back. All of it."

"They don't know who they're messing with," she said, swiping her wine glass from the table. "I've been up against tougher adversaries than these jerks. I fought cancer with my parents, damn it, and they both lived longer than the doctors predicted."

"You're a tough cookie."

"We need to come up with a plan, figure out how to find Nate, extricate ourselves from this mess and get my money back."

"Maybe you should eat something first."

"Good idea, where's the chocolate? I need to dip it."

"On the counter in the white bag."

"Then you know what I'll do?" she continued, ambling into her kitchen.

You'd never know she'd been traumatized by an intruder, or had temporarily lost her life savings. God, he admired her guts.

"What will you do, ma'am?"

"I'm going to cleanse that jerk's negative energy from my apartment by burning a sage stick. Only…"

"What?"

"How do I keep him from coming back?"

"I'm in the security business. Let me handle it."

SYD HAD NO IDEA WHEN Dalton said he'd handle her security issue that he meant he'd assign himself as her bodyguard and spend the night on her sofa.

At least she had two bathrooms, she mused as she got out of the shower the next morning. There was something about sharing that kind of private space with the man that exposed her in a way she didn't welcome, even though she was growing to like the guy and welcome his strength.

She wouldn't grow to like him too much. She knew this was a pit stop, a week out of his exciting life as a government agent, to find his baby brother.

She stared at her reflection in the mirror, the intruder's words taunting her: *Your boyfriend sends his regards.*

No, no and absolutely not. She did not believe that Nathaniel was involved in any wrongdoing. He was a sweet kid, more interested in the latest comic book release than politics. That was one of the things she'd enjoyed about him: his innocence.

Either her attacker was lying or some very bad guys had Nate. She quickly dressed, dried her blond hair and pinned it at the base of her neck with a clip. The thought of Nathaniel being kidnapped and his mind being violated sent a shiver of fear through her body.

Marching down the hall to the living room, it hit her that her predicament was minor compared to what could happen if the country's enemies manipulated Nathaniel's brilliance.

"We need to figure out—" Her voice caught in her throat at the sight of Dalton, sprawled on her sofa, naked from the waist up.

One arm was flung across his eyes as if to block out the light streaming in from the living room sheers. She couldn't help but admire the well-defined pecs and firm abs, lightly dusted with soft, brown hair.

Frozen for a second, she shoved back the lust building in her chest. Heck, this was normal for a healthy young woman approaching her thirties who'd led a relatively celibate life thanks to being a caregiver. She hadn't minded missing out on that kind of thing at the time, but now resented her body's overreaction to the sight of the half-naked warrior.

She could hardly believe this hard-bodied man was related to the skinny and uncoordinated Nathaniel.

She felt guilty salivating over him, but felt even more guilt about waking him when he'd been up all night standing guard.

She tiptoed over to the window to pull the shades.

"I'm awake," he said.

Ah, did he know she'd been watching him? Embarrassment flooded her cheeks.

"How about coffee?" she said, rushing into the kitchen. It was Saturday, technically a day off, yet she and Dalton had a lot to do.

"What were you saying before, about figuring something out?" he asked.

When he sat up she noticed his dog tags fell to the middle of his chest.

"You still wear those, even though you're not in the army anymore?"

"It helps me remember who I am."

She had a feeling it was going to take a lot more than a cup of coffee to make him expand on that comment. He rubbed his temples with his fingertips.

"Headache?"

"Kind of. I don't sleep well in strange places."

"I'm sorry."

"Don't be. Every place seems strange to me." He shook his head as if freeing it of morning cobwebs. "What do we have to figure out?"

"The accounts your brother was most recently working on. What if he innocently thinks he's working on a program for Locke, but he's being manipulated into doing something more sinister?"

"He'd be an easy mark, wouldn't he?"

"Very. And if the bad guys—pardon the expression but I haven't a clue who we're dealing with here—convinced him they were trustworthy, they could basically control your brother. Heck, he could think he was playing some sort of video game and could be breaking all kinds of top secret codes or something."

"Top secret codes?" He eyed her.

"Nate and I used to play Master Code Breaker online."

Even with little sleep she recognized that his eyes shone a blue-green that reminded her of the waters off the shore of Maui. Not that she'd seen them in person. Yet.

"Hold that thought." He went into the bathroom.

She sighed and pulled two mugs off the rack. Although neither of them had consumed much wine last night, she'd had enough to make her relax after her harrowing experience. She'd opened up a little, told Dalton more about his brother. She sensed he wanted to know him better.

"That's sweet," she said, then caught herself. *Girl, this man isn't sweet, he's a government agent, trained to destroy anyone who got in the way of his mission.* At least that's how Nate had described Dalton.

Since she and Dalton had the same mission, she didn't have to worry about being hurt by him. She went to her computer to check e-mail. That gave her an idea. She could access Nathaniel's work e-mail since she knew his password. Maybe his e-mail history would reveal something, give them a lead to help solve this puzzle.

The bathroom door opened and Dalton came out, drying his face with a towel.

"I've signed on to Nathaniel's work e-mail to do some digging."

"You know his password?"

"Yep." She scanned the subject lines and her eyes caught on one that read: Special Assignment.

She opened the e-mail from Arthur Locke inviting Nathaniel to work on a special project at the Locke compound, a mansion overlooking Lake Washington.

"Wow," she said.

"What, wow?"

"Arthur Locke invited Nathaniel to work on a special project at the compound? That rarely happens. Even to someone as smart as your brother." She glanced at him, trying to focus on his eyes, not his broad, tempting chest.

"I did some digging, too," he said. "Apparently, Locke has been a person of interest in a highly classified federal investigation."

"What kind of investigation?"

"I'm not sure yet."

"You can't tell me, right, I get it." She snapped her eyes from his chest and focused on the screen. She scrolled down and spotted the confirmation to the Argosy cruise—tonight!

"Rats! I totally forgot about that. The company's hosting a special cruise tonight for the Technology department."

"Are you going?"

"I'd RSVP'd but had forgotten all about it."

He leaned over her shoulder and eyed the screen. "Will Locke be there?"

"He could be."

"Good. I'll go with you to meet all the players. We'll tell them since Nate got called out of town he asked me to accompany you." He smiled. "As your date."

She snapped her gaze from his amazing eyes and studied the screen. A date with Dalton Keen? How would she survive?

"You're okay with that, right?" he asked, as if he'd sensed her trepidation.

"Sure, sure. I'd better check my e-mail." She signed off Nate's account and got into her own.

The first e-mail that popped up was sent from Nathaniel's Space Cadet account. "Dalton, look."

She opened it and held her breath.

Did you find the DVD you were looking for?—Nate

"Your brother did not send this e-mail," she said.

"How do you know?"

"He would never sign his name, *Nate*."

"The sender didn't know that, but wants you to think Nate's okay."

A sick feeling clawed its way up her chest. She hugged herself and leaned back in her chair. "I'm really worried about him."

"Yeah, me, too."

THE SHARP PAIN OF Broken ribs arced across his chest as Nate struggled to suck in a shallow breath. He wished he could stay in that other world, the one of legends and princesses where he slayed dragons and ruled the Nashadon Kingdom.

Instead, he opened his eyes. Make that one eye since the right eye was mostly swollen shut. Nothing had changed. He still lay on a thin, flat mattress in a cement cell waiting for his next interrogation.

He wouldn't make it through another one.

The door opened and the giant with the meat mallet hands hovered in the doorway. Nate had nothing left, no fear to set his body trembling again, no sense of feeling cold, or hot, or near death.

He was numb. And victorious.

He'd prevented them from breaching the system, even

though Baldie said Nate owed it to them because Nate had discovered the existence of the "death" chip, a chip that could not only be used to control jet engines, but also could be used to get into the government's top security systems. But now, since the government knew of the chip's existence, Locke's "special" team would have to abandon the project.

His brutalizer approached the bed and knelt. With a grip of Nate's chin, the beast turned Nate's face one way then the other.

"Can you see me, pretty boy?"

Nate knew better than to answer.

"I met your girlfriend."

Fury raced through Nate's blood. No, he couldn't mean—

"Sydney Trent?" He smiled. "A hot blonde with sexy eyes and soft, soft skin. I gave her a kiss for you."

With a guttural cry, Nate clamped his hands around the bastard's throat. Nate envisioned his fingers were talons of a great hawk, poised to cut through the man's flesh to prick his carotid artery.

This bastard would not hurt Syd. He couldn't, he—

The brutalizer broke Nate's hold and backhanded him. A sharp, metal ring sliced Nate's cheek and he slammed against the wall, dazed.

"You like to fight, Einstein?"

He grabbed Nate by the arm and slugged him in the gut. Excruciating pain speared through his body.

"Enough!" the bald guy ordered from the doorway.

Brutalizer shoved Nate to the bed. Nate automatically wrapped his arm around his chest and curled into the pain.

"The dork tried to strangle me," Brutalizer said.

Of course he did, the bastard had threatened to hurt Sydney.

"What did you say to him?" Baldie asked.

"I told him I gave his girlfriend a kiss."

Baldie stalked to Nate's bed. There was nothing more they

could do to him. They'd broken his body and threatened his best friend, his FW.

Baldie knelt beside the bed. "Well, if he wants to see his pretty girlfriend again, outside of a coffin, he'll do exactly what we ask." He paused. "Won't you, Mr. Keen?"

Chapter Six

Before they headed to the work party, Dalton called Agent Carter.

"Sir, I was wondering if you could help me out with something."

"Which is?"

"My brother, Nathaniel, is missing. He works for Locke, Inc., a company currently under investigation by the Feds. I need some information about the case, but would rather not go through official channels."

"Do you think he's involved in something he shouldn't be?"

"No," he paused. "Not intentionally. Look, if I find out he is, I'll go straight to Andrews."

"I have your word?"

"Yes, sir. I'm…I'm worried that something has happened to him. He's my only brother and he's a bit naive."

"Okay, I'll look into it. After all, I owe you for being my backup at Pier 69."

Dalton cringed. "Thank you, sir."

Dalton ended the call and glanced out Sydney's living room window overlooking a greenbelt. He hadn't left her side since he'd found her trembling in the hallway last night. He wouldn't risk it, yet he couldn't be her bodyguard forever.

Damn, little brother, what have you gotten yourself into and why drag Sydney into it?

After clearing up the bank account error—the money mysteriously reappeared and Dalton surmised that someone had messed with her funds to make her feel vulnerable—Dalton and Sydney spent the rest of the day going through Nate's apartment looking for clues. They came up empty again.

They stopped by a shopping mall to pick up something for Dalton to wear to the company event. He had a feeling jeans and a T-shirt wouldn't go over well with these corporate bozos, so he let his date pick out his attire, a navy suit, and they headed back to her place.

He smiled at the thought of being her date. Never in his wildest dreams would he imagine dating a sweetheart like Sydney. No, Dalton dated sexual dynamos who were in it for hot, rough sex and a quick exit. It kept life from getting complicated.

"I can't find my cell phone," she said, coming into the living room. She stopped short and eyed him. "Not bad, big brother."

"You picked it out."

"Yeah, but I didn't see it on. The jacket fits good in the shoulders."

She reached out and brushed her hands against the wool jacket. He clenched his jaw. She was assessing him like a prized horse.

Memories flooded his brain. The cheerleaders bidding on him at the high school fund-raiser, wanting his body for the night, but not being interested in anything else. They considered him a prime physical specimen, void of a single intelligent thought. And he'd believed them for so long, all of them. He'd even been jealous of his kid brother for his brains.

The military viewed him the same way: a warrior with the

strength and skill to take down a dozen men, but lacking the strategic ability to plan a rescue on his own.

"You okay?" Syd touched him. This time the touch wasn't one of assessment, but concern.

"I'm fine. You ready?"

"Sure, once I find my phone."

As she moved stacks of magazines and mail in search of her phone, he considered her formfitting black dress. He hadn't noticed her curves before, cloaked in the loose-fitting skirts and sweaters she wore to work. But dressed in the hugging fabric with the low neckline, he found himself wanting to taste the sweet skin of her bare arms, starting with her fingertips, and working his way up to her shoulders and down the front.

"Got it!" she said holding up her phone with a huge smile on her face.

He wanted to kiss her, for no reason other than she was so damn cute.

And your brother's got a crush on her, remember? Do not intentionally walk into a Charlie Foxtrot.

"Let's go," he said, making for the door. He needed fresh air, needed to get away from this girl.

Yeah, buddy, and how are you going to manage that when you're partners in a mission to find your brother?

DALTON ACTED LIKE A jerk ever since she complimented him on the suit. What's the big deal? It's not like she was flirting or anything and even if she were, why would that offend him?

"Introduce me to as many people as you can," Dalton ordered.

"Aye, aye, Captain." She saluted.

"I'm not navy."

"Oh, right."

"I especially need to meet Locke."

They strolled up the wooden pier to the boat, aglow with small, white lights. He offered his arm to escort her.

"You sure?" she asked.

"Of course, why not?"

She slipped her arm through his. "You've been squirrelly ever since we left my apartment."

"I'm focused."

"Sure, I buy that."

"Hey, Syd!" Pete Desai called from the deck of the cruiser.

"Hi, Pete." She waved and shot him a big smile. "That's Pete Desai," she said to Dalton. "One of your brother's work associates."

"A friend?"

"Ah, I guess. They played Warlords game online, but didn't do much else that I know of."

They stepped onto the boat and she noticed Angela sneer in Syd's direction, probably because Syd said she wasn't interested in Dalton. And she wasn't, not like that.

"Sydney?" Alan came up to them, eyeing Dalton. "Mr. Keen. I didn't expect to see you tonight."

They shook hands, and Syd noticed Alan wince at the strength of Dalton's grip. She bit back a smile.

"Since my brother couldn't be here to escort Miss Trent, he asked me to do the honors."

"How gallant," Alan said. "Sydney, I have a business matter to discuss with you, if you can abandon your date for a moment?" He looked at Dalton as if asking permission.

"Sure." Dalton smiled at Syd. "Something to drink?"

"A glass of Riesling, please."

With a nod, Dalton went to the bar where Angela made her

move. She sauntered over to him and beamed an X-rated smile complete with wetting of the lips. What did Syd care?

"Have you heard from Nate today?" Alan asked.

She sensed he already knew the answer.

"Yes, I got an e-mail asking if I found the DVD I was looking for."

"And did you?"

Interesting. Why did he care about an *X-Men* DVD?

"Nope," she lied, but wasn't sure why. *Follow your instinct, girl.*

"Nate asked you to bring his brother to this function?"

He started to lead her away from the group, but she stopped short. Alan was giving her the creeps, even more so than usual.

"I think Nathaniel feels bad that he's not here to hang out with Dalton and he figured since we're friends, Dalton and I could be friends."

Sounded dorky, but she was growing more nervous.

Alan swallowed half of his drink. "Are they close, Nate and his brother?"

"Very." Lie number two. They hardly knew each other. But Alan's attitude was making her feisty. She found herself wanting to mess with his head.

"I hear he works for the U.S.G.S.?"

She had no idea what he was talking about. "I don't know, actually. We haven't talked much about his work."

Dalton caught her eye, and she tried sending a mental message to save her. Unfortunately, Angela continued to blind him with a hair toss and effusive laugh.

"What *have* you talked about?" Alan leaned closer.

Luckily, Drew Crane ambled toward them, but must have read something in Alan's expression because the junior techie slowed down as he approached. She jumped at the chance for rescue.

"Drew! Did the PowerPoint work out?" She stepped away from Alan and he gripped her arm.

She looked into his cold, black eyes, clenched her jaw and sent *him* a mental message: *Don't mess with me, jerk.*

"I'm not done talking to you," Alan said.

"Yes, you are. And if you don't let go of my arm I'll go to personnel first thing Monday morning to file a complaint."

He released her and she breezed up to Drew. "So, did you wow accounting with your brilliance?"

"My meeting isn't until Monday." He eyed Alan, and then glanced at Syd. "You okay?"

She led him away. "Yeah." A nervous laugh escaped her lips. "Alan needs to start drinking cranberry juice, straight, no rocks."

Drew burst out laughing. "You should suggest it in his next review."

Locke was big on supervisors reviewing employees and employees returning the favor with their heartfelt reviews. Only, Syd hadn't developed enough confidence to let her superior know what she thought about his inappropriate drinking and sleazy comments. She'd ignored it up to this point because he hadn't aimed his remarks at her. And truly, his remarks hadn't been flirtatious as much as threatening. Maybe it was time to talk to Beverly in Human Resources.

"Looks like Angela got her hook into some fresh meat." Drew said nodding toward Dalton, who smiled at something Angela uttered.

"She works fast," Syd commented.

A server passed by with a tray of champagne glasses and she grabbed one.

"That's Nate's brother?" Drew asked.

"Yep."

"I never would have guessed."

"Me neither."

"He's big."

"Yep."

"Probably dumb as a box of rocks, right?" he asked, hopeful. Drew was tall, skinny and creative.

"Actually, no. Looks can be deceiving."

Dalton made his way to Syd with Angela panting alongside him.

"Everything okay?" he said, studying her.

"Fabulous."

"I got your wine." He offered her a glass.

"I have champagne. Dalton, this is Drew Crane, one of Nate's friends."

They shook hands.

"I see you've met Angela," Syd said.

The girl smirked. Duh. Well, if Dalton was stupid enough to fall for the busty broad, then he could have her. Sure, why not? Syd sensed he was the type of guy to bed 'em and leave 'em.

Sydney had more respect for relationships than that.

"What brings you to Seattle?" Drew asked, sipping his cola.

"Wanted some time with my brother before I head out on my next assignment."

"He works for the U.S.G.S.," Syd offered, then noticed Dalton's puzzled expression. He'd never given her an official cover story about his job, but Alan had discovered it.

"If you'll excuse us," Dalton said, taking Syd's arm. "I'd promised my brother to meet as many of his coworkers as possible."

"Sure, have fun," Drew said.

Angela slipped something into his suit coat pocket and patted it with manicured fingers. "Those hot spots in Seattle you'd asked for."

Hot spots? Sure, her apartment, her bed, her sofa. Ugh. The

woman made it obvious she looked forward to one-on-one attention later tonight.

Dalton escorted Syd to the other side of the boat through a group of accounting department employees. She introduced him as they passed, but the bean counters didn't have much recollection of Nathaniel.

She and Dalton found a quiet corner of the boat.

"Sydney? Why did you say I worked for the United States Geological Survey?" Dalton asked.

"Alan mentioned it. I assumed that was your cover for what you really do."

His amazing blue-green eyes widened. "My brother told you what I *really* do?"

"He hinted at it. Said you were with a government agency, top secret, spy stuff."

With a sigh, he gazed across Lake Washington to the east side of Seattle. "The U.S.G.S. is my deep cover. The only way you get there is if you've breached the first line of defense."

"Meaning what?" She finished her champagne.

"It means Alan had someone dig awfully deep into my life." He glanced at her. "What else did he say?"

"He asked if you and Nathaniel were close."

"And you said?"

"I said you were very close."

"Even though you know we're not?"

She leaned against the railing. "Alan's been creeping me out lately. Instinct told me to lie."

"Good instinct."

"Yeah, says the guy who has none."

"Excuse me?"

"Angela? You really bought her 'look at my boobs' act?"

"You're jealous?" He smiled, his cheek dimpling.

"No." She glanced across the boat to see who Angela was

going after next. Syd spotted the founder himself, Arthur Locke, stepping onto the boat.

"Hey, that's him, Arthur Locke. I wasn't sure he'd show up."

Syd studied the distinguished-looking multibillionaire with white-silver hair. An aura of power surrounded him, as did two bodyguards.

"I need an introduction," Dalton said.

"Good luck with that. I'm sure he doesn't know who I am."

Arthur Locke walked straight toward them, shaking a few hands along the way. A tall, lean bodyguard hovered by the exit, while the other, a bald, older gentleman with an angular face and serious expression, stuck close to Mr. Locke. Sydney had never seen either of the men before.

Mr. Locke approached Syd and Dalton. "Good evening." He extended his hand and Sydney shook it.

"Mr. Locke. It's an honor to meet you," she said.

"Ms. Trent."

"You know me?" she let slip.

He smiled. "Of course. You keep my IT department fully functional. They'd be lost without you. As a matter of fact, Nathaniel Keen raves about the good work you do."

"Speaking of which, this is his brother, Dalton," she introduced.

"Nice to meet you, sir." Dalton shook his hand.

"Glad you could join us in your brother's absence. I've assigned him to a critical project, but he should be returning in a few weeks."

Dalton sized up Arthur Locke: rich, brilliant, manipulative and evil. There was no doubt in Dalton's mind.

"This is my assistant, Stewart Pratt," Locke said, introducing the bald bodyguard.

Dalton shook his hand, noticing the firm grip. He'd bet the guy was ex-military.

"Nice to meet you, Mr. Pratt," Dalton said.

"I see the resemblance."

"You know my brother?"

"Yes. I work security at the Locke compound where your brother started work on his current project."

"The compound?" Dalton asked.

"Actually, in about five minutes you'll be able to see it from the boat," Locke boasted. "Sydney, you be sure to point it out to Mr. Keen. Nice to see you both."

Dalton watched Locke make his way around the boat, charming staff with his charisma, free food and drink. A few times the bodyguard glanced at Dalton.

"Wow," Sydney said.

"Don't be star struck."

"Says the man who panted at Angela's feet."

"Point out the Locke compound."

"Aye, aye—oops, forgot. Yes, sir." She made for the port side of the boat, grabbing a second glass of champagne on her way.

"Careful with that," Dalton warned.

"Now you're my father?" She shook her head.

Dalton grabbed a quiche appetizer from a waiter's tray and eyed it. He could use a steak, medium rare.

"There, see the lights?" She pointed to the shore. "That's it."

He stroked his clean-shaven chin. "Wish I was navy," he muttered.

"Wait a minute. You're not thinking what I think you're thinking," she said.

He spotted Locke's bald security goon come up behind her.

"You're going to try and swim—"

Dalton shoved the quiche in her mouth. Okay, not the smoothest move, but he didn't know how else to shut her up.

She'd figured out he was planning to swim the frigid lake if necessary to access the compound and find evidence about his brother's disappearance. Hell, maybe his brother was still there. He didn't need Sydney broadcasting his plan to Locke security.

She swallowed the quiche and whacked him with her small purse. "That was seafood. What if I was allergic to seafood?"

"Excuse me," the bald bodyguard said, stepping closer. "We're taking pictures for the employee newsletter. How about one of you two on the dance floor?"

"I don't—"

"Sure," Dalton interrupted her, wanting to get away from the guy.

Dalton took her champagne glass and handed it to the bodyguard, then led her to the dance floor where couples were swaying back and forth to a slow song.

"I can't believe you shoved that in my mouth," she said.

"Locke's man was right behind you and you were about to broadcast my intentions."

She leaned back. "You aren't really going to—"

He pressed his forefinger to her lips. "I have no food to shove in that pretty mouth of yours so you'd better watch it or I'll have to kiss you."

Her violet eyes widened as if the thought terrified her. Or excited her. He couldn't deal with either option at the moment.

He guided her head to his chest and moved in sync with the music, struggling to remember the last time he held a woman like this, with one hand to her waist and the other at the small of her back. She slipped her hands around his waist and he liked the feeling of being clung to, as if she relied on him, needed him.

Yeah, don't forget your brother is relying on you to save his ass.

And he would. But he wanted to enjoy this brief moment with this gentle girl in his arms.

"Mr. Keen?" a man asked.

Dalton glanced up as a photographer snapped a picture.

"Hey, I wasn't smiling." Syd shot him a broad smile and he snapped a second shot.

Dalton wanted to rip the camera from the guy's hands and toss it into the lake. Dalton's job was to be stealth so they didn't see him coming when he breached security to save hostages. He didn't need his picture showing up in the company newsletter or on the Internet or anyplace, for that matter. He'd have to retrieve the memory card from the guy before the night was over.

He guided Syd's head to his chest again and resumed the slow dance. To an observer, he and Syd looked like a couple in love. He gave himself a mental slap.

Instinct told him his brother was in trouble and Locke and his men were responsible.

"Locke knows where Nate is."

She tilted her head back to look at him. "Huh?"

"So does his bodyguard. I'll bet my pension the kid isn't overseas on business."

"Then, what's it about?"

"My guess is they're involved in something illegal and are using my brother's intelligence to achieve their goal."

"Poor Nathaniel."

Her tone was not one of a woman missing her boyfriend, but that of a concerned big sister.

"What do we do?" she asked.

"I'll get into the mansion and look for evidence of his whereabouts."

"But if you're caught—"

"Let's talk about it later." He closed his eyes, enjoying the feel of her silken hair against his lips.

Snap out of it, Keen, or all three of you will end up dead. At the hand of Arthur Locke's men.

Dalton would call Zack Carter tomorrow to see if he'd unearthed anything helpful.

He glanced up and spotted seductive Angela sauntering toward him planning to cut in. Instinct warned him not to leave Sydney alone with Arthur Locke or any of his people. How was he going to convince Syd not to go into work until this situation was resolved?

More importantly, how was he going convince Angela to keep her distance? The flirt closed in, her eyes widening with desire and her jaw set with determination.

"Syd?" he whispered.

"Uh-huh?"

He sensed she was feeling a little buzzed from the champagne. Good, maybe she wouldn't nail him with a karate kick after what he was about to do.

"I'm sorry, kid," he said. "But I going to have to kiss you."

She straightened, but before she could protest he cupped her chin between his forefinger and thumb.

Tipped her head.

And tasted the most amazing girl he'd ever kissed.

PRETEND YOU'RE BROKEN. Pretend you're on their side.

Nate had changed his tact due to the threat against Sydney. It wasn't fair that his intelligence and curiosity put her life at risk.

Nate had to figure his way out of this mess and protect her. First, he'd convince them he needed access to the Internet so he could send an encrypted message to Sydney, the one person he knew could decode his gibberish. If the message was intercepted, it would be meaningless to his captors.

Although his captors had managed to send a crippling virus to Homeland Security, they weren't able to fully access the top secret security systems, like INXP.

Baldie had given Nate a laptop and loose fitting sweat-pants as a reward for breaking into Baldie's ex-wife's e-mail and accounts. It had been a test, one small job to prove Nate's ability to breach a secure system. Small potatoes.

He wondered what would be next?

Doesn't matter. He'd cooperate, get access to the web, and send Syd an S.O.S.

The door opened and Baldie walked in, laughing. "I sent out fifty pornographic e-mails from the slutty ex-wife's e-mail address and emptied her savings account. Lord, it has been a good day."

Guilt tore at Nate. He'd caused an innocent woman to lose her life savings to this sonofabitch.

There'd be worse losses at the hands of these bastards.

"Such fun, such fun," Baldie said. "You've earned another reward."

"A shirt?" Nate asked. The chill was getting to him.

"No, but cook has made you something special." A short, middle-aged woman brought in a tray with an aluminum cover over a plate.

Nate's mouth watered. He'd been living on stale crackers and water since they'd locked him up three days ago.

She opened the cover to reveal a peanut butter and jelly sandwich. Nate fought back the urge to grab it and shove it in his mouth as he watched the woman set down the tray nearby.

The woman and Baldie started for the door. "Oh, I almost forgot." He tossed a manila envelope to Nate's cot. "Some reading material."

"I don't suppose I could get access to the Internet?"

Baldie narrowed his eyes. "Pants, a laptop and a sandwich aren't enough?"

Baldie snatched the plate from his tray and handed it to the woman, leaving only a carton of milk.

"Wait," Nate said.

Baldie glared. "What?"

"I'm sorry," Nate said, glancing at the floor, feeling shamed and helpless.

"So am I."

"But—"

"Shut up or I'll take back your pants, as well."

Nate leaned against the wall. The door closed with a deafening click. He opened the envelope with trembling fingers. He might be malnourished, but he shouldn't be trembling like this, should he?

He slipped photos from the envelope and froze at the sight of Sydney, *his Sydney*, in his brother's arms.

"Syd?" he whispered.

He looked at the next color photo, then the next. His brother and Nate's best friend, Nate's FW, were dancing without a care for anything but each other.

Without a care for Nate.

He flipped to the last picture: Sydney and Dalton kissing.

Nate was being starved, tortured and made to do things against his own country.

Yet no one cared.

He was alone, betrayed by the people who were supposed to care about him the most. He closed his eyes and struggled to hang on to a shred of hope, but he couldn't find one.

Chapter Seven

The next day as they boarded the motorboat at Yarrow Bay Marina, Syd fought a mild hangover from the bubbly last night. It didn't help that she got little sleep thanks to Nate's hunky brother stretched out on her sofa. She kept having dreams of Dalton slipping under the sheets, kissing her neck, her shoulder, her breasts.

She shivered.

"You cold?" he asked, offering his hand to help her into the boat.

She clenched her jaw and stepped into the boat without his help. Touching him was *not* a good idea.

"I'm fine," she said, sitting in the passenger seat.

He grabbed the cooler from the dock. "I said I was sorry."

"You don't have to apologize." Which he had. He'd apologized at least four times since the amazing kiss that left her fantasizing about him all night.

"You're still mad at me about the kiss, but I explained. I had to stop Angela from cutting in."

"I know, I know. I'm not mad. Drop it. But tell me one more time why you're breaking into the compound in broad daylight?" She zipped up her fleece to guard against the cool, fall weather.

He pulled away from the dock. "Locke left the state last night on business. He's due back tomorrow night. There's usually less staff when he's out of town."

"How do you know that?"

He shot her a charming smile as if to say he knew everything, about everyone, thanks to his spy job.

"Oh, right."

She glanced at the horizon, feeling a tad woozy. How much did Dalton know about her, she wondered? He knew how to hold her and how to kiss her. She'd never been kissed like that. It had been so unexpected from the tough soldier. She figured his kisses would be aggressive. Yet he was gentle, as if he was treasuring her lips, wanting to remember their taste until the next time.

Uh, no way, girl. There can be no next time.

This situation was complicated enough with her job on the line, Nate missing and her bank accounts in flux. She didn't need to add an impossible relationship into the mix.

"You're too quiet," he pronounced.

"A little hungover."

"I warned you."

"Blah, blah, blah," she said, glancing at the floating bridge in the distance. The one thing she didn't need was the I-told-you-so lecture, especially since he was partly the cause of her hangover. She'd initially grabbed the champagne to lighten up, shake off the jealously building in her chest at the sight of Dalton and Angela.

Okay, how mature was that?

"How long do you think it'll take?" she asked.

"An hour, tops. I'll drop anchor two properties away and swim onto the compound."

"How are you going to get past security?"

"I'm talented."

That smile again.

Something tingled between her legs. Good grief.

"What?" he said.

"I'm worried."

"Thanks, but I'll be fine."

"And if you're caught?"

"I won't get caught."

An odd expression creased his forehead.

Then she remembered Nathaniel mentioning that his brother had been sent to Port Townsend to rest and recover from a particularly gruesome assignment.

"Why did they send you out here?" she asked.

"To recuperate."

"From what?"

He glanced over his shoulder and winked.

"It's classified?" she guessed.

"Yep."

"Were you hurt?"

He looked away, eyeing the waterfront. "Yep."

"Were you caught by the bad guys?"

"You could say that."

"Did they hurt you?"

He sighed, but didn't answer. She read pain in his expression, pain and regret.

"Sorry," she said.

"You have no reason to apologize."

But she'd caused that pain in his eyes. If she hadn't brought it up, hadn't pushed—

"I was caught, tortured and nearly killed. Worse, I trusted the wrong person and almost got a hostage killed."

"A hostage's life is more important than yours?" She didn't get it.

"Yes. Which is why it's so important for me to find Nate.

He isn't just a hostage, he's my kid brother and I feel responsible for him."

"We don't even know if he's being held against his will."

"You can say that after the odd things that have happened the past few days?"

"I guess not. Enjoying a moment of denial, I suppose."

"The moment's over." He nodded toward shore. "There it is." He cut the engine and dropped anchor.

He pulled off his jacket and ripped his shirt over his head exposing his bare, amazing chest. He smiled and she realized she was gawking.

"Sorry," she said, analyzing her fingernails, the polish chipped in about four different places.

"Stop apologizing," he said, slipping a wet suit over his swimsuit. "I'm the one who dragged you into this mess and kissed you against your will."

She shrugged.

He eyed the shoreline. "My target spot is actually two properties north of the compound. I'll be back in an hour, probably sooner."

"But what if you're not?"

"I'll be back, I promise." He went to the edge of the boat.

He was about to drop into the dark, cold waters of Lake Washington, break into the mansion of a man who became a multibillionaire by designing security systems.

"Dalton, wait." She touched his shoulder and he turned to her.

"Be careful." She stood on tiptoe and kissed him. Not sure why, but it seemed like the right thing to do. He gently gripped her shoulders and it felt good, make that great.

He broke the kiss. "We seriously have to stop doing that," he said with a smile. "But it's too much fun. You behave. I'll be right back."

He shoved his mouthpiece in place, grabbed his waterproof bag of supplies, and dropped into the water.

In seconds he was swallowed by the dark green, bottomless mass and she squinted to see him, but he'd gone too deep.

A big cruiser whooshed past, sending obnoxious waves her way. As the rented boat pitched, she collapsed to the bench seat, struggling to keep her equilibrium.

Talk about throwing off her equilibrium, that kiss hadn't helped matters. Why did she kiss him? He'd said it himself: because it's fun. But so unlike her.

Girl, you should be worried about what happens if he doesn't return and you're alone on this mission to find Nate and free yourself from this intrigue. She needed Dalton, she admitted to herself.

But did she need him for security or something more?

IT WAS TOO DAMN EASY, Dalton thought, shoving the tank and wet suit into the bushes of an older, neighboring property whose owners were out of the country for a few months.

The lake hadn't been as cold as he'd expected thanks to the wet suit, and the swim actually felt refreshing. Once on land, he'd changed into his clothes and started toward the Locke property. According to Zack Carter, security was lax until you reached the house. Dalton checked his watch. He had a few minutes to wait until Carter sent the glitch to disarm the security system allowing Dalton access.

Truth was, he had a hard time focusing after Syd kissed him. He'd have a talk with her when he got back, explain that he wasn't a relationship type of guy, and that she deserved better.

He realized she'd kissed him because she was scared of being abandoned, left alone to figure her way out of this mess. For a sweet kid like Sydney, that had to be scary as hell.

But he wasn't leaving her alone. Not anytime soon.

Eventually, well…

His watch alarm vibrated. He had ten seconds until security was down.

He closed in on the house.

Eight seconds.

He found cover behind a thick rhododendron bush as the camera swung his way.

Six seconds.

Had to get closer, make his way to the garage since Intel indicated this was the best spot to penetrate security and get into the house.

Four.

The camera swung left and Dalton raced to the lower-level garage door. *Breathe. Focus.*

He took out his pick.

Two…one.

His watch vibrated again, he heard the door click and he made quick time on the lock. Once inside, he slipped past three fancy sports cars and opened the door to the lower level. Fluorescents lit the long, white hallway. He made his way up a level of stairs and followed the small diagram Carter had given him with the location of Locke's home office: second floor, new wing, northwest corner overlooking the lake. The east wing was the original structure, built in the forties.

Gripping his Glock between his hands and pressing his back against he wall, Dalton climbed to the second level. Coming out a few feet from Locke's office, he eyed the cameras. Hopefully Carter's plan had worked and the signal would be scrambled for a good ten minutes, which gave Dalton maybe seven to go digging.

He slipped into the billionaire's office and shut the door. Holstering his gun, he went through the desk first. Then his eyes caught on a security monitor of four areas of the house.

On one of the screens, his brother was sitting at a table playing cards with half a dozen men. They were laughing and drinking, smoking cigars. Nate sipped what Dalton figured was whiskey from his glass.

This was a man who was shy and uncomfortable around people? He looked like he was having a night out with the boys.

Dalton's gaze drifted to another screen: a bruiser body-guard stood outside Locke's office door.

"Damn," he swore.

Dalton rushed to the door and waited. It swung open, slowly, the barrel of a gun poking through the door.

Dalton knocked the weapon from Bruiser's hand, but the goon swung his other fist around to connect with Dalton's cheek.

Dalton struggled to focus through stars that crossed his vision and pointed his gun at Bruiser.

"Breaking and entering is a criminal offense," Bruiser said with a smirk.

Dalton wondered how many other Bruiser-types were on their way.

"I'm here for my brother."

"He's on assignment. Likes it where he's at."

"I don't believe you."

Bruiser shrugged.

Dalton wanted an easy way out: no cops, no attention. "Give me your security card."

Bruiser tossed a card onto the desk, and then put up his hands. As Dalton reached for the keycard, Bruiser flung something at Dalton that sliced through his shirt, cutting his arm.

Dalton stumbled back in shock. Bruiser rammed his shoulder into Dalton's stomach, once, twice. Dalton couldn't breathe, but he wasn't letting go of the gun. He pounded the butt of the gun against the back of the guy's head until Bruiser stumbled back, dazed.

Struggling to catch his breath, Dalton whipped open the door and raced downstairs, using Bruiser's card to open the doors. But it didn't work on the door to the outside. Leaning against a Jaguar in the garage, Dalton pulled out his gun and fired at the lock on the garage door, annihilating it. He kicked open the door and raced across the property. He found it odd that no security alarms had gone off which meant he was still within his ten minutes of security system shutdown.

"I'm not done with you, Keen!" Bruiser shouted.

He sounded about fifty yards away. Dalton had a good enough lead. He kept running, ignoring the blood seeping down his arm and dripping off his fingertips.

Why did he use a silent weapon? Why not shoot Dalton?

Because there'd be too many questions.

Dalton realized he didn't have time to change into the wet suit and put on the air tank. He was going to have to swim without equipment.

He wondered how far he'd get.

He kicked off his gym shoes and dove into the lake, the frigid water shocking the breath from his lungs. Without the wet suit, it felt like he was swimming in an ice bath.

He stayed under as long as he could, but surfaced for another breath.

"There's big brother!" Bruiser called.

Dalton submerged.

And was nailed in the shoulder by a knife. Every stroke shot pain down his body. He couldn't remove the object from his shoulder; had to get back to the boat, to Syd.

Damn, what if they followed him back to her?

He stuck to the shoreline, hoping Bruiser would lose sight of him, or think Dalton was dead from the knife wound.

When Dalton came up for air again, the sickening laughter of Bruiser echoed in the distance.

But he didn't hear a boat motor. Okay, so the guy wasn't following him.

Why?

Focus on getting to the boat, getting the knife out of your back, and not succumbing to hypothermia.

His strokes were slower than usual, what with the loss of blood and ice water stiffening his muscles.

One more stroke, another, one more.

His mind started to wander, images flooded his brain. Images of failed missions, the hell of basic training, the taste of Sydney's lips.

Okay, he was completely losing it. He surfaced and spotted Sydney in the distance. Far off, every time he surfaced she seemed farther away.

Another stroke, come on, one more.

Couldn't focus, ringing in his ears grew louder. He was going to pass out, damn it.

"No," he groaned. He recited the pledge of allegiance in his head to keep focused. Over and over, had to stay focused, stay conscious. His brother was missing.

Sitting at a table with a bunch of guys, laughing, partying. Not like him. Not like Nate.

You don't even know him, a voice taunted.

He wouldn't get to know him if Dalton drowned in Lake Washington.

I pledge allegiance to the flag of the United States…

His country. Served his country. Killed for his country. So much death.

He was swimming in it. Couldn't get away. It was everywhere.

And it was swallowing him whole.

His arms stopped moving.

His mind shut down. Turning over, he floated on his back, drifting across the mass of death.

His heartbeat pounded in his ears. Slower, slower…

I'm sorry, Nate. God, kid, I'm sorry.

"Dalton, get up here!" a woman's voice ordered.

Something poked him, caught on his shirt and dragged him across the water.

"Get in the dang boat," she demanded.

He looked into the most amazing shade of purple eyes, beautiful eyes on a sweet, heart-shaped face.

"Knife," he said, but his voice was hoarse.

"Come on, turn over so I can help you into the boat." Dalton gripped the side of the boat, but didn't think he had the arm strength to pull himself up.

He sunk, but she grabbed his shirt collar and pulled him to the side of the boat. With a jerk, he broke through the surface.

"Grab the rail and climb up the ladder," Sydney commanded him.

With his left hand, he gripped the rail. Pain from the knife wound surged through his back when he tried pulling himself up.

The woman yanked him onto the boat. He was careful to land on his side. "Knife," he muttered. "Back."

His body trembled, trying to warm itself.

"It's not there," the woman said.

Woman? What was her name again? "Sydney?"

"You need out of these wet clothes."

Hands lifted his shirt up and over his head. He groaned against the pain of the shoulder wound. No knife? He must have worked it out as he swam away.

"What the heck happened?" she asked, slipping off his pants.

"Got into the house. Bodyguard caught me."

"Did they follow you?" She pulled out a first-aid kit.

"Don't think so."

"Sit up and let me take a look." He felt something press against his shoulder. He hissed through clenched teeth.

"Sorry. I'll put a bandage on this for now, but I think you need stitches."

Stitches, he'd had those before. No problem.

A minute later she wrapped a blanket across his shoulders. "Where else are you hurt?"

"Arm...bleeding."

"I'll fix it."

She pressed something to his arm as he drifted in and out of consciousness. When he opened his eyes she smiled at him.

"I'm hot," he said. "Blanket off."

She swore under her breath and gripped his chin. "Dalton, I need you to do something. Can you touch your pinky to your thumb like this?"

He watched her and looked at his right hand, struggling to make sense of what she wanted him to do. Opening his hand he struggled but couldn't imitate what she'd done.

"I'm, I'm trying," he said.

"Shh, it's okay."

He recognized panic in her voice. It was not okay.

"Nate, I saw him," he blurted out.

"Shh, it's okay. I'm going to get us away from here."

A few seconds later they were speeding across the lake, the wind sending chills through his body. Yet he was hot, and ripped off the blanket. Didn't help. Sunlight poked through the clouds, blinding him. He closed his eyes.

They stopped, drifted, rocked back and forth.

"You need to lie flat." She coaxed him to lie down. He pinched his eyes shut against the sun, still feeling the wet death clinging to his skin.

Would he ever get it off?

Then something else touched his skin, something that felt like soft, warm clouds. It felt like heaven.

Contentment filled his chest. The clouds destroyed the wet death, cooled him off. And he wanted to stay this way. Forever.

Chapter Eight

A high-pitched beeping sound shocked Dalton into consciousness. He lay practically naked with a woman on top of
him, also mostly naked. Where the hell was he?

The beeping shocked him out of his stupor. It was a special
tone designed to let him know when he'd been called by his C.O.

He reached for his pack and the girl scrambled off him,
taking the blanket with her.

"Syd?" He sat up, looked around and groaned as pain shot
across his back. He reached around and felt a bandage there.

He blinked, trying to get his bearings. He and Syd had
been lying naked in a boat. *Remember, damn it.*

"It's okay," Syd said from beneath the blanket, which
she'd draped over her head.

Her petite hands grabbed her clothes and they disappeared
beneath the blanketed mass.

"If you're conscious, you must be better," she said.

"What happened?"

She slid the blanket off her head and eyed him. "You
don't remember?"

He shook his head, ready to apologize: for taking advantage of her, for forgetting what surely must have been the
most amazing sex of his life.

"You broke into the Locke compound and were caught."

It all rushed back: the bruiser slamming the wind out him, the knife in the back…the sight of Nate hanging out with a group of guys on the security feed.

"Yeah, okay. I've got it now."

"Good." She disappeared beneath the blanket again.

He searched the immediate area and found his duffel bag with a dry shirt and jeans. He slipped the shirt over his head.

"But Syd?"

She ripped off the blanket to reveal a fully dressed, adorable blonde. "Yeah?"

"You were naked. On top of me. Or did I imagine that?"

She blushed, then tipped up her chin. "You were going into stage two hypothermia. My best weapon was the warmth of my body."

"Oh, okay." For a second he wished she'd taken advantage of him.

Yeah, while he was suffering from hypothermia? *Sick, sick man.*

"We'd better head back," she said, pulling up anchor.

The sun blazed bright yellow from the west side of Lake Washington. Hell, how long had they been out here?

He got dressed, shifted onto the bench seat and checked voice mail.

"Agent Keen, this is C.O. Andrews. I need to speak to you ASAP. I'm calling at seventeen hundred hours."

"How long was I out?" he asked.

"A few hours?"

He nodded and called in. "Commander Andrews, it's Dalton Keen."

"Agent Keen. I have an assignment for you. You leave the day after tomorrow."

Dalton rubbed his forehead.

"I'm sorry, sir, but I can't do that."

"Are you defying an order?" Andrews pressed.

"It's not that I'm defying an order. I want what's best for all involved. I need a few more weeks."

"You mean you're mentally not ready to go back in the field?"

Dalton hesitated. If he said yes, they'd never put him back out there. But what other excuse could he give?

"What's going on, Keen?" his C.O. pushed.

Time to come clean.

"My brother, sir. He's missing. I'm afraid it may have something to do with the microchip case. He's a computer genius so I asked for his input regarding the microchips and I fear he's been kidnapped because of something he stumbled onto."

Dalton was putting his brother before his work, choosing to defy an order so he could find Nate.

"I see," C.O. Andrews said.

"I didn't think I was putting him in danger, sir. At the time, I thought I was helping expedite the mission."

"Do you have a lead on your brother's whereabouts?"

"I think he's being held at Arthur Locke's compound in Kirkland."

"Locke, the security giant?"

"Yes, sir."

"He does work for the military."

"I'm aware of that, sir."

"You're officially on an extended leave, Keen. I'm sorry about your brother, and even sorrier you involved a civilian. After this situation is resolved, you'll need to come to D.C. for a meeting."

In other words, Dalton needed to be fired in person.

"I understand."

"And Keen?"

"Sir?"

"You're welcome to use our resources to help you find him."

That shocked Dalton.

"Thank you. I appreciate that, sir." He shoved the phone into his jeans pocket.

"Everything okay?" Syd asked.

"Just peachy."

"Oh, boy. That's not good."

"At least I'm alive, thanks to you. How about I buy you dinner?"

"A free meal, sure," she joked.

But they both knew that danger hovered close by. Danger from someone at Locke, Inc., someone who had taken his little brother against his will. Dalton puzzled over the security monitor's image of Nate hanging with the guys. Nate holding a drink in one hand and a cigar in the other.

He didn't drink or smoke. Or did he? Dalton wouldn't know. It was time to get to know his brother as intimately as any hostage.

"I'm going to need your help," he said to Syd.

"No, absolutely not."

"You don't know what I'm going to ask."

"I'm not helping you break into the compound again. I've seen enough blood, thank you very much."

He stepped up beside her. "I need you to help me understand my brother. It's the best way I can help him."

"Oh, okay, I can do that. You up to navigating us into the marina?"

"Sure." He grabbed the wheel. "And thanks, for patching me up."

"You should see a doctor."

"I should do a lot of things."

AN HOUR LATER THEY were back at Syd's place. They'd decided her first aid was good enough since the wounds weren't deep, and she'd given him some over-the-counter pain meds.

They sat at her kitchen table with containers of Thai takeout. She'd had a hard time keeping eye contact, still embarrassed that she'd pressed her naked body against his.

You saved his life, girl. Get over yourself.

Dalton knew her motivations were honorable. He didn't think she was trying to seduce him. For Pete's sake, the guy was in la-la land.

"You want pad thai?" he asked, sliding the box over to her.

"Yeah, thanks."

She scooped a heaping of noodles onto her plate.

"Sydney, I have another favor to ask of you."

She shoved the noodle dish back in his direction. "You ask a lot of favors. I'm keeping track."

"You do that. This is a biggie."

"Uh-oh, what?"

"I don't want you to go to work."

She leaned back in her chair. "For how long?"

"Until we resolve this situation."

"I can't quit my job."

The thought killed her appetite. She'd picked the job because of its stock options and travel benefits. Without it, she'd have to wait that much longer to take her dream trip.

If she'd learned anything from her parents' deaths it was not to wait to follow your bliss. Life was unpredictable.

"Syd, I didn't say quit," Dalton leveled her with bloodshot eyes. "I said don't go to work."

"They can fire me for that."

"Not if you're sick, or you have a family emergency."

"I have no family, remember?" She crossed her arms over her chest, depressed at the reality she was all alone.

"Does your boss know that?"

She considered his question. Except for her relationship with Nathaniel, she'd kept her private life private. She didn't talk about her parents or the fact she had only one sister who was way too involved in her own personal dramas to be interested in Syd's life.

"They probably did a background check on me."

"Do you have any living relatives?"

"A sister outside of Portland."

"Good, your sister needs you. Call it in first thing tomorrow morning."

"I don't know, Dalton." She stabbed at her noodles with the chopsticks.

Dalton shifted to the chair beside her and touched her hand. She stared at his strong yet gentle fingers that warmed her skin.

"Syd?"

She glanced into his colorful eyes.

"Something's not right at Locke. I don't know what it is, but everything in my being screams that it's dangerous. They've got my brother and I won't let them get you. Understand?"

She sighed. For a second she felt like he cared about what happened to her. She'd floated off into fantasyland, riding into the sunset with this handsome prince.

But he wasn't a prince. Dalton was an agent who'd disappear into the mist, leaving her alone. Again.

Still, she appreciated the feeling of someone caring. That had always been *her* role.

"I'll call in a family emergency," she said. "As a matter of fact, I'll call directly to personnel and bypass Alan the jerk."

"Thanks." He exhaled as if he'd been holding his breath.

He ripped his cell from his waist and glanced at the caller ID. "I need to take this."

"Okay."

He paced to the window. "Keen."

She took a bite of pad thai. Dalton's body language made her hesitate mid-chew.

"I can't understand that, sir. No…maybe seven years. Yes, I will. I can find it. Thank you, sir."

Dalton's arm dropped to his side. He flattened his other hand to the wall and bowed his head.

"What?" she asked.

He shook his head.

"Dalton? You're scaring me."

With a sigh he turned to her, his eyes filled with pain. "That was my C.O. He's got proof that my baby brother is a traitor."

HE COULD HARDLY BELIEVE HE UTTERED the words from his own mouth. Nate. A traitor.

"You're wrong," Syd said, standing up and going into the kitchen. She poured herself a glass of water. Yet there was a full glass beside her plate. Dalton figured it was her nervous habit.

"He's being framed," she said, holding the glass. Her hand trembled.

He leaned against the wall, struggling to keep his distance, because right now he could use some warmth from this woman, a connection to chase away the demons about to claw their way through his chest.

His brother was a traitor.

And Dalton was partly to blame. Damn, if he hadn't high-tailed it out of the Keen home after graduation, he could have prevented their bastard father from ripping Nate's psyche to shreds. The kid didn't stand a chance against manipulators like Arthur Locke, who had Nate doing God knows what while telling him he was creating a security system to protect a customer.

"What's the proof?" Sydney challenged.

He hesitated, not wanting to drag her deeper into this.

"Tell me!" she cried, slamming her glass to the counter.

"Does it matter?"

"Apparently not to you. You believe your brother is a traitor, just like that." She snapped her fingers.

"It's not his fault. He was manipulated."

"Stop right there. Nate may be naive and…and flaky, but he isn't stupid. He would never do anything criminal."

Dalton studied the brown carpeting. He sensed her approach, but didn't look up. He couldn't. He felt ashamed that he'd caused this situation, asked Nate to help with a case, opening a Pandora's box. Ashamed that he didn't know his brother well enough to know he'd betray his country, even by accident.

Dalton didn't believe in his scatterbrained genius brother. Talk about betrayal.

Sydney framed his face with her gentle hands. "Look at me, Dalton."

He had no choice but to look into her caring eyes.

"Your brother is not a traitor and he's not *that* gullible. You have to believe in his goodness. He's in trouble and he needs us."

"Yeah, we'll find him."

"Because he's your brother."

"Because it's my job. He's now a person of interest in an NSA investigation."

"No." She stepped back. "We're not going to find him because your job requires it. We're going to find him because he's your baby brother and needs your help. What is the matter with you?"

"I can't ignore the facts. There's evidence of tampering with the government's mainframe security system. My brother is one of three guys who could break into that system. They've checked out the other two. They're clean."

"Stop it. Stop talking like a machine and think about Nathaniel. How can you believe he would do this?"

"Because he's my brother."

"Meaning?" she pushed.

He turned away from her and glanced out the window at the starlit sky.

"He's your brother, meaning what?"

"Did Nate ever talk about our father?"

"No."

"Well the old man was a sonofabitch who bullied and emotionally beat us into submission. At least he tried. I got the hell out before I lost all self-confidence. But Nate…"

"Nate, what?"

"Nate took the brunt of it. He coped by shutting down. But deep down he's desperate for approval from a strong male. He probably gave in hoping to get that approval."

She planted her hands to her hips. "Nathaniel is not a weak kid looking for approval. He's smart and kind, and a little scatterbrained, sure, but he's not a defenseless victim."

"Then the alternative is that he joined this conspiracy willingly."

"Shut up."

"Excuse me?"

"Eat your dinner." She marched back to the table.

He stared at her.

"Come on." She motioned for him to sit. "Eat so we can get down to business."

"What business?"

"The business of you getting to know your brother."

SYDNEY SPENT THE REST OF THE EVENING acquainting Dalton with his brother. She showed him Nathaniel's playful e-mails and watched video from their day spent at Mount Rainier. She and Dalton ended up at Olympic Sculpture Park in Seattle, one of Nathaniel's favorite spots to sit and think.

Luckily Dalton's injuries weren't serious, yet she insisted he take a pain reliever. She suspected he was used to being in pain and wasn't very good at taking care of himself.

Watch it, girl. You need to focus on taking care of yourself, not this lost soul.

She and Dalton settled on a metal bench overlooking Puget Sound.

"Your brother is kind and smart and sometimes silly," she said. "But he is not a criminal and doesn't have a mean bone in his scrawny body."

Dalton stared across the still water.

"You're still not convinced?" she pushed, zipping up her fleece.

"What do you want me to say?"

"That you're going to put your family before your job."

"My job," he chuckled.

"I missed the joke."

"I screwed up and involved a civilian—Nate—on the last mission. I'll be out of a job when this is over."

"Good, family should come before everything else."

"Not my family."

She stood and glared at him. "Look, get over it already. Life deals us some crappy situations. Your mean dad, my parents dying before they got to see their grandchildren. Move on already."

She started for the car, irritated that she'd lost her temper, but more irritated that she cared so much about Dalton that she wanted him to heal from his past.

He'd never heal as long as he clung to his pain.

He caught up to her. "Hang on a second."

"Coward," she muttered.

"What did you call me?" He stepped in front of her.

"You heard me. You're a coward because you're not willing to let go of your past. You hang on to it like a shield of protection, but it's not protecting you, Dalton. It's robbing you of true happiness."

She stepped around him and got to the car, frustrated that she'd wasted three hours of her life on a man who wasn't listening. Sticking her key in the door lock, she noticed he'd answered his cell phone. Oh, sweet chili peppers. It was probably another call from his boss with more bad news and lies about Nathaniel.

Getting into the car, she felt her cell phone vibrate. She dug it out of her pocket and read a text message.

Got away from kidnappers. Need help. Meet
at gazebo, Marina Park, Midnight. X

"Nate," she whispered. He was okay, and needed her help.

The passenger door swung open and Dalton got into the car. "Thanks for the education, but that was my boss. The Feds have issued a warrant for my brother's arrest. I can't protect him anymore. The only hope of keeping my job is to help them find my brother and bring him in for questioning."

She hit the End button on her cell and slipped it into her pocket. "I'm sorry to hear that."

He touched her shoulder and she closed her eyes. Oh,

fiddle fudge. She wanted this man to be her partner, not her enemy. But he'd made his choice.

"I'm sorry my brother dragged you into this mess," he said.

"It's not his fault. But you can't see past your guilt to believe that, so I'm not talking to you."

"Syd, listen—"

"Stop, just stop talking. I'm tired and I've wasted three hours of my life on a man who's incapable of seeing the goodness in his own brother."

The words were harsh, especially for Syd.

"Who sent you a text?" he asked.

She snapped her gaze to meet his. "What?"

"I saw you looking at your phone. Who was it?"

Dalton's suspicious tone rankled her.

"I didn't get a text. I sent one."

"To whom?"

"A friend," she said, pulling onto First Avenue.

"If it's Nate, you need to tell me."

Sydney was sweet and kind and hated lying above all else. But she'd do anything to help Nathaniel, who'd been abandoned by the one person who was supposed to believe in him.

"I sent a text to Drew telling him I won't be in the office tomorrow in case he needed me to help with his presentation."

Out of the corner of her eye she could tell he studied her to determine if she was telling the truth.

"I resent your tone," she said. "Just because you see enemies everywhere doesn't mean your friends are all enemies."

He glanced out the front window. "Is that what we are, Syd? Are we friends?"

"I guess not. My mistake."

That shut him down. Good. She needed to keep her distance from this sexy, but disappointing man. The self-centered jerk was abandoning his little brother. Syd wouldn't. She'd help Nathaniel and in the process dig herself out of this mess.

Just not with the help of the hunk sitting next to her. Now to figure out how to sneak out with Dalton keeping guard on her living room sofa.

You can do it, girl. You have to.

"HOW'S OUR PROJECT coming along?" Arthur Locke asked over the speakerphone.

"Excellent, sir," Stewart Pratt said. "Einstein Corp. is close to solving the software challenge."

"What's taking so long?"

Pratt ground his teeth. They'd had the kid for less than a week and Locke expected him to be broken already?

"Complications. We're smoothing them over with help from a female consultant."

"I need closure by the end of the week."

"You'll have it, sir. We've laid out the details, made our offer and are retaining the consultant tonight to help finish the deal."

"I'll be back the day after tomorrow, late evening."

Which meant Locke expected progress by then.

"Yes, sir." Pratt clicked off the phone and eyed the security monitor.

The wimp, Nathaniel lay curled up on his cot, shivering.

Pratt ripped the radio from his belt. "Roy?"

A second passed. "Yes, sir?"

"Wake him. I'm coming down."

"Yes, sir."

Pratt tapped at the screen with the antenna of his radio. "Why won't you fully break, punk?"

He considered using hallucinogens, but didn't want to screw with the kid's brain too much for fear he wouldn't be able to do his magic and break into INXP, the government's top secret mainframe that only a handful of people knew about.

And Pratt was one of them, thanks to his work for the CIA.

The kid turned over in his sleep as if fighting off a nightmare.

"Oh, son, it's only the beginning." The kid was more than halfway gone, stripped of his will to think for himself or defend himself.

The give-and-take relationship had worked well up to this point. Pratt had given him a shirt last night and the kid acted as if he'd been given a new sports car. Yes, they were close, but the genius was unpredictable.

And they were running out of time, which was why Pratt needed an ace in the hole. They'd kidnap the girl and threaten to kill her in front of him unless boy genius followed orders.

It was all coming together. The system would be breached and Locke, Inc. would ride up as the savior, with the program to lock out all further attacks, while having access to it all.

The kid would be tagged with the crime, along with his co-conspirator, Sydney Trent.

Nathaniel's big brother would be left, wondering what the hell had happened to his life. He'd lose his job, his brother, and a woman Keen had assigned himself to protect. The former Special Ops agent would be gutted from the inside out.

Locke and his team would be on top, the heroes, with their own agenda.

"We're almost there," he said, eyeing the kid, who tossed onto his back. "Now to work on you."

Chapter Nine

Sydney paced within the gazebo, wondering if it might be better to hide behind a post rather than expose herself like this.

Guilt tugged at her conscience for putting the Valerian root tincture in Dalton's drink, but she rationalized it would help him sleep and heal from his injuries.

Duh, now she was lying to herself. She wanted him to sleep through tonight's adventure because if she told him what she was planning to do he'd tag along and arrest his little brother.

So, she'd spiked his drink, locked Storm in the bedroom and slipped out at eleven-forty.

She checked her watch. It read twelve-ten. "Come on, Nathaniel."

It dawned on her how quiet the lakefront was at this time of night other than the faint music from a restaurant in the distance. She felt very alone out here.

A patrol car cruised past.

And stopped.

Uh-oh.

When the cop got out of his car she went to greet him.

"Good evening," the Kirkland patrolman said eyeing her all black outfit.

Dress for the occasion, right?

"Hello. Beautiful night," she commented.

"May I ask why you're out here this late at night?"

"I'm waiting for my boyfriend. He said to meet him here at midnight, that he had something important to discuss." She quirked her eyebrows.

"Kind of an isolated place to be waiting."

"Don't worry, I'm prepared for anything." She slipped her high-grade pepper spray from her bag.

"Yeah, well, be sure not to use that stuff on your boyfriend or he might forget what he wanted to talk to you about."

She chuckled. "Right, good advice."

"Take care, miss."

"Thanks."

Friendly cop got into his squad car and pulled away.

Gripping the pepper spray, she went back to the gazebo, worried that something had happened to Nate, that they'd caught him again. She wished she knew who "they" were. Could Locke really be behind this intrigue?

"Sydney!" Nate called out in a panicked voice she'd never heard before.

"Nate?" She turned to the source of the sound. Something rattled in the bushes behind her.

"I'm here." She rushed to the bushes but slipped on the damp earth, landing on her rump.

"Sydney!" he cried again.

"Nate, where are you?" She stood and brushed herself off. She'd dropped her pepper spray, darn it.

As she started for the bushes, someone grabbed her from behind. Then she spotted the big guy who'd broken into her apartment coming towards her.

She clicked into self-defense mode and stomped on the attacker's foot. He loosened his hold, she jerked her head back, nailing him in the mouth and broke free. Racing across the park, she wished the friendly officer's timing had been better.

She also wished she'd had better sense than to walk into this trap. But she'd been sure Nate had sent her the text.

A car pulled up to the curb and the door opened. Arthur Locke's bald bodyguard stepped out. "Ms. Trent. I need a word."

"Not on your life, buster." She spun around and raced north, as another car pulled up, blocking her. Bald guy was marching towards her from the east, husky guy coming at her from the west, and mystery car blocked her escape from the north. Two men got out of that car, one holding a video camera of all things!

Anger flooded her chest as she raced from one corner of the park to the other, looking for the weakest point, feeling like a pinball about to drop into a hole.

But this wasn't an arcade game. It was her life, or death.

Nope, no way, not happening. These jerks weren't going to steal her life before she got to travel and experience the world. There could be three or four or even ten of them, but they'd never come up against a furious and determined Sydney Trent.

She raced to the only corner they hadn't covered, and cried out for help.

"Help! Stop! Police!" She knew how her voice carried. Mom and Dad always told her she'd be a great singer if only she could carry a tune.

Instead she'd become a caregiver, friend, and wannabe adventurer.

"Help! Stop! Police!" she cried over and over again.

Footsteps pounded the earth behind her. One of the goons grabbed her arm and spun her around. She kicked husky guy's shin, hard. He gripped her arm tighter and backhanded her across the cheek. She went down, bracing herself with her hand. Damn, that hurt.

She knew from the look in his black eyes that he wanted to kill her. She scooted away from the guy as he towered over her with a horrible, threatening gleam in his eye. Oh, boy, he not only wanted her dead, but he wanted to molest her.

"Keep dreaming, bruiser," she spat.

"Spirited. Must be why pretty boy genius is in love with you."

Her breath caught. Nate?

"Step away from the girl," Dalton ordered, aiming his gun at her attacker.

She struggled to breathe. Dalton was here, saving her.

"Hey, buddy. I thought I'd put you out of commission," her attacker said.

"Hardly." Jerking the barrel of the gun, Dalton motioned for the guy to move away from Syd.

The black limo pulled up to the curb and the door opened. "Get in the car!" a man ordered.

The big guy backed up and smiled at Syd. "Until next time, sweet thing."

He shot Dalton a mock salute, got in the car and took off. It was too dark to see the license plate.

Dalton holstered his gun and knelt beside Sydney.

"You okay, sweetheart?"

"I'm…I'm…"

"Shh." He stroked her hair. "Take a deep breath."

The beep of a siren echoed across the park. Friendly cop had returned.

"Sir, put your hands where I can see them," the cop ordered walking toward them.

"It's okay," she called out to the cop. "My boyfriend showed up in time."

Dalton eyed her. "Your boyfriend?"

The cop approached, hand to his firearm. "What happened, miss?"

"Some guys jumped me. I'm fine."

"You should fill out a report."

"I should get to the emergency room. I think I broke my wrist."

"Can you give me a description?" the officer pressed.

"It all happened so fast. No, not really."

"Regardless, you should file a report."

"I know, tomorrow." She stood and Dalton cupped her elbow. She must have looked bad because of the pained look in his eyes when he studied her face.

"I'll drive her home." Dalton eyed her. "We'll come back for your car tomorrow."

"I'll watch you escort your girlfriend to the car."

"Thanks," Dalton said.

She fought back tears of frustration. She'd looked forward to seeing Nathaniel, making sure he was okay, and putting an end to this mystery. But enemies were everywhere, in the form of Locke employees, and maybe even Nathaniel? Did he send the text to lure her to the park so she'd be kidnapped?

No, she believed in her friend. But she'd heard his voice, which meant they must have recorded it and played it back to lure her into the bushes. She shuddered at the memory of the sound of Nate's desperate and scared voice.

Dalton opened the passenger door and she climbed into his SUV.

She was in no emotional condition to drive, and her wrist wasn't going to function properly for a while.

Dalton closed the car door and came around to sit behind the wheel. He sighed and turned to her.

"Syd, look at me."

She faced him and he winced as he touched her cheek, ever so gently. "Need to get ice on that. How about the wrist? You want to swing by the emergency room?" Concern flooded his blue-green eyes.

She'd never been taken care of before. It felt good. "No, it's a sprain. I've got an ace bandage at home."

"Okay." He glanced at her wrist, then back up to her eyes. "I have something to say." He sighed, then leveled her with an agry glare. "What the hell were you thinking?"

HIS FURIOUS TONE escaped against his will. She could have been abducted, damn it, or worse.

"What was I thinking?" she said, an edge to her voice. "I was thinking that Nate needed me, that he was all alone since his brother had given up on him. I was thinking I could help him escape and get some answers and end this flipping nightmare."

"You are powerless against these people. Don't you get that?" he said.

She stared him down. "No, Dalton. I was powerless against cancer. I'm powerless against random death, but I'm not powerless against these bullies."

He reached out to trace a strand of hair from her eyelash. She turned away from him. "I want to go home."

"We can't."

She squared off at him. "Why not?"

"They're aggressively after you now. They know where you live. We need to find another place to stay for a few days until we work this out."

"What's to prevent them from tracking my credit card receipts and finding us?"

"I'll use one of mine with one of my aliases. But I need to ask you a favor."

"I'm *so* done doing favors for you."

"Hey, I saved your pretty little butt tonight. That at least earns me the right to ask."

"I guess." She crossed her arms over her chest and winced at the pain in her wrist.

"Don't ever lie to me again," he said. "Please?"

"I was trying to help Nathaniel."

"I understand that. Your heart was in the right place."

"But my brain was misplaced, right? Just drive, I want to at least go back home and pick up some clothes."

"Not tonight. Your place is too hot."

She stared out the passenger window.

He headed south toward Bellevue figuring one of the hotel chains would have an opening for a few nights.

"I'll stop by a twenty-four-hour drugstore and get you a wrist bandage."

She didn't respond. Of course not. She was still in shock after having been chased all over the park, and then slapped to the ground.

Dalton tightened his grip on the steering wheel. Sonofabitch. His finger had twitched when he'd pointed his weapon at Bruiser, and not because the guy had nailed him twice earlier today. No, Dalton wanted to kill the guy for touching Syd.

He still couldn't believe she thought she could sneak out unnoticed. Sure, he'd tasted the Valerian in his drink. He'd tried it in the past so he recognized the pungent flavor. But he knew it had little affect on him.

He'd pretended to be asleep to see what she was up to. She'd acted odd ever since she'd received the mysterious text, so after she went to bed he'd planted a tracking device in her wallet, then waited. And sure enough, at eleven-forty she'd sneaked past him for a late night stroll, aka her rendezvous with Nate.

She wasn't meeting up with Nate because she was in love with him. She wanted to help Nate because she knew Dalton wouldn't: he didn't believe in his brother's innocence.

"We need to talk," he said.

"Not in the mood."

A woman not in the mood to talk? There was a first.

"What made you go to the park tonight?" he asked.

"A text from your brother that he'd escaped and needed my help. He signed it *X* so I thought it was legit."

"They probably went through e-mails he'd sent you to figure out how to sound convincing. What did the guys say when they cornered you?"

"Nothing, except," she said, "some guy was taking video. What the hell was that about?"

"I haven't a clue. Tell me more."

"I heard Nate calling my name, but I never saw him. Then they chased me and the big guy hit me. He called me spirited and said that must be why pretty boy genius was in love with me." She sighed. "But I was clear with Nathaniel from the start. I love him as a friend, but could never love him like *that*."

They drove in silence a good ten minutes, Dalton puzzling through what had happened. He'd have to call it in, let his boss know the mystery enemies were after Sydney.

Who believed in Nathaniel's innocence so much that she'd risked her life to help him. If only Dalton could believe.

And why didn't he? Because he was blinded by cynicism and duty and…guilt.

Dalton blamed himself for not protecting Nate as a kid, for not being there when he kissed his first girlfriend, had his first drink. The guilt paralyzed Dalton's ability to see clearly.

Maybe if he took off the blinders he could get a clear look

at what was really happening. He glanced at Sydney, who cradled her wrist in her lap. She was strong and determined and a good judge of character. She'd pegged Angela's motives, knew her boss was dangerous and proclaimed Nate an innocent victim.

What if she was right? What if Dalton's emotional wounds didn't allow him to see the truth?

Syd was so utterly loyal to his brother and Dalton felt a deep, honest connection to her. If she was willing to sacrifice her life for Nate, why couldn't Dalton?

Some guy was taking video...

It hit him square in the chest. If Locke's men wanted to control Nate, and couldn't gain his cooperation through physical torture, what better way than to emotionally break him by showing him video of Sydney being stalked...or molested.

He clenched his jaw. Was that what they'd planned to do? The burn in his chest went way beyond that of hostage rescuer. He had developed real, scary feelings for Sydney.

Bury it deep, Keen. You've got more important issues at hand than your crush on this girl.

Like his brother's survival. Dalton realized Locke's men would use mental torture, an insidious, ugly process, only if the physical torture had failed, which meant...

"Damn it, Nate," he whispered, realizing the pain his brother must be going through at the hands of these monsters.

"He's not the bad guy," Syd said.

"I didn't mean it like that."

"Whatever. I'm tired of arguing with you."

"Good, because from now on we work together."

"Ha, ha. So you can find your brother and arrest him? No thanks. I'm a better friend than that."

"I want to be a better brother, so help me out here. We find him and take him in, for his own damn safety. He's safer in jail than with Locke's men, or out on the streets where they can get to him. Make sense?"

"I guess."

Deep down Dalton guessed Locke's men wouldn't let Nate get anywhere near the Feds…alive. Baby brother could probably take down the entire organization with one click of a computer button. Dalton guessed Nate had been sucked in too deep to ever be free again.

Hostage rescue was Dalton's specialty. He'd figure out how to keep his agency and the Feds off his case long enough to rescue his baby brother and clear his name.

I'm coming, little brother. Hang in there.

Chapter Ten

They settled into a room at the Westin hotel as Mr. and Mrs. Blanchard. He wasn't letting her out of his sight. Now that would be a trick considering he still had to track down and rescue his brother.

Dalton had wrapped ice in a towel and held it to her cheek while they watched late night television. He could tell she avoided going to sleep, probably fearing she'd have nightmares.

Somewhere around eleven she'd drifted off, and he'd climbed into the other queen bed and struggled to relax. Not easy with adrenaline rushing through his body.

"Stay away," she whispered.

Dalton sat up, and watched her. He couldn't sleep. Not when he knew she replayed the scene from earlier tonight in her dreams.

"Nathaniel," she whispered.

He told himself there was no romantic edge to her voice, but could he trust his own judgment? Didn't matter. She was a genuinely honest girl and if she said she considered Nate nothing more than a friend, Dalton had to believe her.

She'd made him leave the bathroom light on in case she awakened and was disoriented. From the glow of the light he watched her thrash beneath the white sheets. It was driving him nuts and he knew how to fix it. Which would drive him even more nuts.

"Hell." He stretched out on top of the sheets, held her and stroked her hair. "Shh."

She settled a bit, and then froze. Uh-oh.

With a hand to his chest she pushed up. "You're in bed with me."

"You were having a nightmare. I'm on top of the sheets. Come on, lie down."

"But, but you climbed into bed with me."

He could tell she was half-asleep. "Yep, I did. Now lie down so we can both get some rest. We've got a lot to do tomorrow."

"What day is tomorrow?"

"Monday."

"Work."

"No work, remember?"

"No, I'm confused," she said, her voice trembling.

"You're still asleep. Lie down." He patted his undershirt. "Syd, please?"

She snuggled up against him and gripped his shirt above his heart.

Aw, damn. Even though his shoulder wound ached and his arm stung from being sliced by Bruiser, Dalton felt more comfortable than he had in years.

Because she lay against him, breathed against him.

Needed him.

Yeah, you wait, buddy. Once this is over, she's out of your life, so don't lose your head.

Unfortunately he was dangerously close to losing his heart.

SYDNEY WASN'T USED to waking up next to a warm body, especially not a solid one like Dalton's. She freaked at first, then remembered the nightmare of being chased, caught, hurt…and Dalton coming to her rescue, lying beside her and soothing her to sleep.

He had stroked her hair with such a gentle, yet assured touch. All fear had fled from her body and she had drifted off, the nightmare turning into a dream of her and Dalton kissing, touching and holding each other.

She fully opened her eyes and leaned on an upturned palm. His eyes were still closed, his breathing slow and steady. And his lips? His lips tempted her, as she remembered their taste.

She started to lean forward and caught herself. This was not her boyfriend. He was a secret agent, out to rid his conscience of guilt for abandoning his brother when they were kids.

She hopped out of bed and made for the bathroom.

"What's wrong?" he asked, his voice thick with sleep.

"Have to use the potty." She didn't know what else to say to get away from temptation, from the need to kiss those incredible lips.

Inappropriate!

She locked the bathroom door, splayed her hands across the sink and stared at her reflection. What was the matter with her? Wasn't it obvious? She ached to have a man in her bed, to wake up in strong, male arms, to be soothed to sleep.

To be loved.

"Not yet, there's no time for that," she scolded her reflection.

She had oceans to swim, mountains to climb, villages to explore.

But first she had to get her life back, and the only one who could help her was the hunk lying in the next room. She needed Dalton to help regain her freedom, that's all.

She turned on the shower, filling the room with warmth and realized how cold she felt after leaving his bed. Ooh, she needed to focus on not getting used to him being around, holding her and chasing away her nightmares.

Maybe she should reconsider dating a nice man who could accompany her on her adventures and warm her bed. Why did she sound so clinical about it?

Dalton knocked on the door and she cracked it open.

"You need clothes," he said, not looking at her. "I'm going across to the mall. Size six?"

"Eight is better," she said, appreciating the compliment.

"Lock up behind me." He turned and held her gaze. "Do not answer the door for anyone. I have a key. I'll put the Do Not Disturb sign out so housekeeping leaves you alone."

She stepped out of the bathroom and followed him to the door. He turned abruptly and she nearly collided with his chest.

"No one, hear me?" he said, pinning her with those amazing eyes.

"Yes, sir." She saluted with a grin.

"You're so damn cute." He leaned forward and kissed her on the forehead.

Grr. She didn't want to be cute this morning. She wanted to be hot and sexy, to be someone this hunk wanted to kiss on the lips. He pulled the door closed and she locked it from the inside, flipping the security bar.

After a long shower, she wrapped a towel around her hair, one around her body and went to watch television. It was odd how the world could look so normal, when she was embroiled in chaos thanks to Nate and his sexy brother.

She watched a morning talk show while towel-drying her hair. That's when she thought she heard a knock at the door.

She muted the TV and waited.

Another knock.

Relax, they can't get in without a key, and even then—

The key card clicked. She scrambled behind the bed, out of sight.

The door opened and hooked on the security device.

"Syd, open up," Dalton said.

With a relieved sigh she let him in. "You scared me out of my wits."

"Sorry," he said, glancing nervously around the room as if seeing her in a towel was making him uncomfortable.

"Check this out." He plopped a shopping bag from Macy's on the bed. "I got pants, tops, socks, didn't know what to do about shoes, oh, yeah, and this stuff." He plucked panties from the bag with a forefinger and thumb.

"I'll take that *stuff*, thanks."

"I also got one of these." He shrugged a pack off his back.

"We are going hiking?" she said, analyzing the clothes.

"I got us an untraceable laptop so we can fly under the radar."

"And where are we flying to?"

"Locke, Inc.'s business systems. We're going to dig for clues to Nate's whereabouts."

"I thought you said he was at the compound."

"He was, but I don't know if he still is. I think they set me up to see him sitting with the guys playing cards. Thought I might leave it alone, I don't know," he said, his voice trailing off as if he still puzzled over his brother's role in this mystery. "Anyway, Locke's got a private plane. We can check manifests, e-mails, even phone records."

"You can break into phone records?"

"Uh…not officially." He smiled and set up the laptop at the table.

Syd went into the bathroom to change and was pleasantly surprised at the clothes he'd picked out for her: hip-hugging jeans and a deep rose, jewel-toned cotton shirt. She dressed, and pulled out one more thing, a black denim jacket. "He's got some style," she said, surprised that a man like Dalton would know what would look good on her.

She opened the door and started to thank him, but stopped short at the tone in his voice.

"You can't expect me to sit here and wait," he said to someone on his cell phone. "Yes, I understand, sir but…Which is my point. If anyone is going to risk his life, it should be me…yes…I will." He tossed the phone to the bed, crossed his arms over his chest and stared out the window.

"What happened?" she asked, coming up beside him.

"I've been ordered by my C.O. to stay out of the investigation. He won't risk losing agents because I've lost my perspective."

"I'm sorry." She touched his shoulder, but he didn't seem to notice.

"So I'm stuck here, in this hotel room, babysitting you until it's over."

"I didn't realize I was that much of a pain."

He turned to her, his eyes softening. "You know that's not what I meant."

She smiled.

"You're messing with me?" he asked.

"Maybe."

He glanced back outside.

"I hate seeing you so torn up and restless," she said. "There's got to be something we can do to help this along."

"Follow orders. That's what a good soldier does."

"Huh. Don't you ever get tired of being good?" She paused. "Cuz I know I do."

"Really?" He narrowed his eyes at her.

"Ooh, I just flirted with you, didn't I?"

"Maybe."

She put out her hands. "Didn't mean to, sorry. But sometimes I want to do what I want to do without worrying about how it's going to affect twenty-seven other people. Oh, never mind, I sound scatty. You can still do a little Internet digging, right? I mean you won't be leaving me alone. You'll still be here, in this room."

"I shouldn't."

"It will make the time go faster. Did your boss give you an idea about how they were going to find Nathaniel?"

"They're doing a full background workup on Locke."

"Okay, in the meantime, we could do a little e-mail investigation." She sat at the table and placed her fingers to the new laptop. "We'll start with Alan's e-mails. He knows something or he wouldn't be acting so creepy."

"While you do that I'll call my friend Griff to see if he can dig up something on Locke."

"Is Griff another agent?"

"Former agent."

Dalton called his friend and Syd used her pass code key to get into Alan's work e-mails. At first nothing jumped out at her, but then her eye caught on an e-mail with her name in the subject line.

It was sent from Stewart Pratt's and read:

Situation will be resolved tonight.

Which was last night. Which meant her boss knew about her planned abduction.

"I can't believe this!" She stood and motioned at Dalton to get his attention. He put a finger up as if to say he was deep in conversation.

Her cell vibrated, buzzing across the nightstand. She grabbed it and recognized Alan's phone number. The bastard. She wanted to answer it and give him hell, but then he'd know she'd busted into his computer files. That would get her fired for sure.

Girl, you've got more to worry about than being fired.

She let his call go to voice mail. She paced the room half listening to Dalton speak to his agent friend.

Her cell vibrated again. "Jerk," she muttered. "He won't give up."

She eyed the caller ID. This time it read the HR department at Locke. She nibbled at her lower lip. What if Alan had spread lies to Beverly in Human Resources? What if they were talking about Syd, discussing how to terminate her?

"Sydney Trent," she answered.

"Sydney? It's Alan."

Sneaky, calling from Beverly's line.

"I left you a message that I'm having a family crisis, Alan. I can't talk." But she wanted to, she wanted to rip him a new one.

"Oh, so you haven't heard?"

"Heard what?"

"Turn on the midday news. I'm so sorry."

The line went dead. "Ick, ick, triple ick," she said, dropping the phone like it was on fire.

"What?" Dalton asked, shoving his phone into the holder on his belt.

"My boss is creeping me out. He said to turn on the news." She shuddered, then aimed the remote and hit the On button.

A special report filled the screen about a multicar crash, burning metal and lost lives. "Tragic," she said. "But why…?"

Her voice caught in her throat. There, on the screen, flashed a photograph of Nathaniel with his playful smile and unruly hair falling across his forehead. The broadcaster said something about victims.

Dead victims.

To destroy them, you must become them. Then you will earn their trust.

Nate remembered the phrase from Warrior Kings IV, a game

he and Drew used to play online. Nate wouldn't become one of these bastards, but if he could convince them of his loyalty, they would trust him and give him an opportunity to escape.

He'd played along yesterday by drinking and gambling with the guys, while he secretly assessed the older east wing of the mansion where they held Nate prisoner.

The bald bastard had awakened Nate four times during the night, using sleep deprivation and mental games to break Nate's will. If Nate didn't break from his father's mental torture, he surely wouldn't break from this idiot's assault.

On the contrary, the more his body weakened and his mind raced, the more determined he became to beat these monsters, and play some mind games of his own.

He'd start by offering a taste of the ultimate power by accessing the Secretary of Defense's private e-mail. Under Nate's watchful eye he'd give them the ability to read private documents meant for those with the highest security clearances. Nate would create a bug to break the connection after five minutes. He'd act frustrated and angry and say he needed more time with the program to work out the kinks.

He was a genius, after all, and they were just bullies with money.

As he suspected, Baldie came back an hour after his last visit and sat in a chair across the room.

"How are you feeling this morning?"

"Fine, sir." Nate sat up in bed. "I've been thinking about that program you wanted me to design to access the Secretary of State's private computer. I've got it figured out in my head, but could use a notebook, Internet access and some coffee." Nate smiled, acting like one of the team.

"Internet access again?"

"I'll need to test the system, sir. You can be right beside me when I test it."

"You're awfully cooperative today."

"Why wouldn't I be? You've offered to pay me a ridiculous amount of money to design software. That's my job, isn't it?"

Baldie leaned back and crossed his arms over his chest. "You've almost convinced me, son."

"I'm sorry?"

"Why the sudden change of heart?" Baldie pushed.

"You're right, sir. This country is in serious trouble. Only a true leader like Arthur Locke can make it right and bring peace and balance to the United States of America."

The whispers, a form of brainwashing, had been piped into his cell throughout the night. Nate never thought the skills he'd developed to shut out his father could save his mind and his life.

"How about a test?" Baldie got up and opened the door, motioning for someone to join them. Meat Mallet Man wheeled in a television and plugged it in.

"I want to show you something." Baldie hit a button and played video of Sydney crying out for help as Meat Mallet Man and his thugs chased her around the park.

Lock it up, Nate. If they think you care, you're back to square one.

Nate stripped himself of all affect and stared at the screen, acting as if he watched a cereal commercial. Syd's screams cut through his chest, piercing his heart as if someone was shoving an ice pick between his ribs.

Fifteen seconds passed and Meat Mallet Man turned off the television. Nate glanced from the bruiser to Baldie.

"Why did you show me that?" Nate asked.

"Did it bother you?" Baldie pushed.

"She's betrayed me and is in love with my brother. Why would I care what happens to that bitch?"

Baldie smiled at the big guy.

"So, did she live up to your expectations?" Nate asked Meat Mallet Man, not sure how he'd control himself when the bastard answered.

"The bitch got away."

"Figures," Nate said, biting back his joy. "She's a sneaky one."

"Do you still want her? Maybe teach her a lesson?" Baldie asked. "We could have something arranged."

He'd wanted Syd since the first day he'd caught her fighting with the photocopy machine. Nate knew she deserved better. She deserved a compassionate, healthy and protective man. Not a selfish wimp like Nate.

"I want something more exciting than Miss Goody Two-shoes," Nate scoffed. "Besides, I don't want my brother's hand-me-downs."

"Well, son," Baldie said, "you get us started on Phase I of the INXP project and we'll send someone to visit you tonight."

Damn, they were going to send him a prostitute and expect him to perform in his weakened state? Sure, they probably looked forward to watching.

Baldie extended his hand. "I look forward to working with you."

They shook, but Nate's grip was purposely weak. *Always appear weak so your enemy won't see it coming.*

"We'll prepare your upstairs accommodations and move you later today. I apologize that it's still in the old part of the mansion, but it's definitely a step up from the basement."

The men started for the door, but Baldie hesitated and turned back to Nate. "Oh, and one last thing. We'll be changing your name since you're officially dead."

"No kidding?" Panic filled his chest at the thought of

everyone giving up the search for him. *Yeah, buddy, who is "everyone"? Syd and Dalton had already moved on.*

"We've officially killed you off so you could start fresh. Things were getting messy at work. The Feds issued an arrest warrant for you. Now that you're dead, you're safe."

"Thank you, sir. I appreciate everything you've done for me, sir."

"My pleasure, son."

Anger flooded Nate's chest. Son?

"What's my new name?" Nate asked.

"We'll let you choose."

"Do you have a favorite?" Nate asked Baldie. *That's it, bow to your master.*

Baldie studied him and said, "Jonas. How about Jonas Meyers?"

"Sounds good, sir. Thank you."

"Get some rest. We'll wake you when we're ready to move you upstairs."

Nate lay down and pulled the blanket over his shoulder.

"See," Baldie whispered to the big guy. "Breaking wills is much more effective than breaking ribs."

"How do we know he isn't faking it?"

"We will know after my one last test."

Chapter Eleven

The air rushed from Dalton's lungs as he stared at the screen, struggling to make out the words uttered by the newscaster.

Nate's youthful face flashed on the television, his eyes crinkling at the corners with his infections grin. Dalton was going to be sick.

"No, it's not possible," Sydney said.

Syd's voice sounded far away, drowned out by the guilty cries of Dalton's conscience.

You couldn't help him and now he's dead.

"I don't understand," he muttered.

Deep down it was all too clear: the bad guys had won. They'd kidnapped Dalton's brother and had gotten what they needed from him. To cover their tracks, they set up a car accident to burn the evidence of physical torture.

His brother, the naive, gentle Nate, had been tortured beyond repair.

"Sonofabitch!" He grabbed a chair and smashed it against the television, trying to break the hold the newscaster's voice had over his soul. A sob racked from his chest as he fought back the anguish of losing his brother before he could make things right.

He tossed the chair to the other side of the room. The buzz

of silence filled his head. Silence was better than the sound of the newscaster's voice:

> …a three-car accident on 405…one dead, two injured…a man believed to be an employee of corporate giant Locke, Inc.…

Dalton massaged his temples with his palms and went into the bathroom. He flipped on the cold water, struggling against embarrassment, grief and rage. They all fought for the top spot in his brain as he splashed water on his face to get his bearings.

His brother was dead because of something Dalton involved him in. That was why they'd gone after Nate, right? Because of the microchip that Dalton had shown his brother?

Here all he wanted to do was mend a torn relationship, develop an understanding and appreciation between brothers, maybe even learn to love his brother who was so much his opposite. A brother who'd suffered at the hands of their abusive father because Dalton had been a coward and ran to the army for cover.

Admit it. You wanted to make it up to him. You wanted his forgiveness.

And now he'd never have it.

"Sonofabitch," he swore again, fighting back a sob of grief. He would not cry, he would not allow himself that luxury.

"It might be his car, but they can't know Nate was behind the wheel," Sydney said from the doorway.

"Leave me alone."

"No."

He turned to her, furious that she was challenging him. "No? My brother is dead and you can't give me space?" He stormed past her, feeling caged in.

"He's not dead. They wouldn't kill him."

He spun on her. "And how would you know that? Are you a government agent or cop? No, you're a secretary. You know nothing."

Instead of hurt spreading across that sweet face, she narrowed her eyes in anger. "Go ahead, be nasty, be rude. Do whatever you have to do to move past this."

"Past it? My brother is dead."

"I refuse to accept that and so should you."

"Are you nuts? Is that why he liked you so much? Because you're living in fantasyland just like the kid was?"

"Stop and think for half a second." She paced to the window and back to the bathroom.

Back and forth, tapping her forefinger to her lips, as if struggling to remember the answer to a trivia question.

"We both know he was kidnapped by Locke. Locke even admitted Nate was working on a project for the company. Then you see him on the TV monitor in Locke's office. This is too neat." She stopped and stared him down. "He's not dead. They're faking us out."

"It's his car. They found his body. It will be confirmed in a few days when they do the autopsy."

"It makes no sense. You know why?"

He shrugged.

"Nathaniel never takes 405. He hates the traffic and makes it a challenge to find his way around the east side using side streets. I don't believe it. Uh-uh. Besides, why would they kill him?"

He gripped her shoulders, staring deep into her beautiful eyes. "They got what they needed from him. And you know how?" He leaned close, his lips brushing against her hair. "They tortured him, tortured him so severely that questions would be asked if anybody found his body. So they destroyed it, burned it to ash. My brother, my baby brother."

With a defensive move, she broke his hold and shoved at his chest. He stumbled back, in shock.

"Snap out of it! The pity party is over, Keen. Do your job as a big brother and figure out what's really happening here."

"I know what happened. It's over." He ambled toward the window, but she stepped in front of him.

"Yeah? Why was he driving on 405? His car had been sitting at his apartment complex, right? When did he get it? And where was he going? We knew he'd been kidnapped, and suddenly he's alone, in his car, on 405?"

"Maybe he was trying to escape." He glanced out the window at the same expressway where his brother was killed.

"He'd get in touch with us. He wouldn't do this on his own. Come on, get your stuff. We're going for supplies." She grabbed her purse and jacket.

"What are you doing?" he asked.

"We're going to the drugstore for some poster board and markers."

"But I…I have to call my mother, make arrangements."

"We're not giving up. We have work to do. Shelve the grief and let's go."

Dalton followed her out the door, numb, unable to think past his next step down the hotel's carpeted hallway. So many conflicting messages, so many raw emotions, and he couldn't process a single thing.

He felt weak and deflated. Even though this girl beamed with hope, Dalton knew she was in denial mode, putting off the inevitable.

In the not-too-distant future, Dalton would be burying his baby brother.

SYDNEY DRAGGED DALTON to the drugstore and back to the hotel room carrying three bags of supplies. She was humming with nervous energy, determined to prove Dalton and the news reports wrong: Nathaniel was still alive. She wouldn't accept anything else.

A few hours later she'd created a basic outline of the last few days on poster board. When she was confronted with a puzzle, she needed to "map it out" as her tutor had taught her in grade school. If she drew things, she could make better sense of them.

"We've started at the beginning and worked our way across the continuum." She drew a star on the left hand side of the board.

Dalton wasn't listening. Instead, he had stared out the window for hours at the passing cars. She wondered if he was slipping into shock. Here was a guy who'd seen gruesome violence at the hands of his enemies, yet he'd completely shut down at the news about Nathaniel. It was then she realized Dalton loved his brother. Deeply.

And she was falling in love with Dalton.

Shelve it girl! The last thing you need is to introduce that dangerous emotion into this mess.

"So, I started with the last time I heard from Nathaniel which was Friday, September 14." She made a mark on the timeline. "Then you showed up on Friday the 21. Immediately after your arrival, Alan announced that Nathaniel was sent overseas, which was the first I'd heard of it," she muttered. "Then Alan threatens my job because of my personal relationship with Nathaniel. Nathaniel was either in trouble from day one or something happened right around the time you showed up. What do you think?"

He didn't respond.

"Dalton?"

He glanced at her.

"What made you come looking for him?" she pushed.

"I hadn't heard from him in a while."

"You hadn't heard from him before and didn't come looking for him. What else is going on here?"

"I involved him in something I shouldn't have. And now he's dead."

"Stop it." She tossed a glass of water in his face.

He blinked, his eyes widening in shock as droplets clung to his lashes. "You threw water at me."

"I had to do something to snap you out of your coma. Now focus." She studied her poster.

"Why are you doing this?"

His tone scared her. She didn't look up for fear she'd see tears in his eyes. She couldn't handle that, not from this powerful man.

"He's not dead," she said. "I'd know it if he were dead."

"Why can't you accept it?"

She pointed a marker at him. "You know why? Because I've seen death take too many lives too soon. I won't give up without a fight. There's no DNA on Nathaniel, no real proof. We know Locke had him working on something scary as hell so I wouldn't put anything past them to cook up this story to stop us from looking for your brother." She refocused on the poster board. "Are you going to help me or what?"

She wrote down another clue, the scary beast waiting for her in her apartment. The same beast who'd accosted her at the park.

Dalton came up behind her and touched her hair. "What are you about, Sydney Trent?"

She sighed. "I'm about life."

"So you are," he whispered in her ear, then kissed her cheek.

She almost melted into a puddle, but they didn't have time for that. Locke's bad guys wanted her and Dalton to think Nathaniel was dead. Where did that leave Sydney? Afloat without an oar, that's where.

Dalton took the seat across the table from her. "What is all this?"

"A time line. See how it all fits together? And yesterday." She pointed with the marker. "You saw your brother on the monitor. That's the most concrete information we have. How did he look?"

"Like a man drinking with his buddies."

"Drinking?"

"Yeah, they were sitting around a table, gambling, drinking and smoking cigars."

"Okay, I'll flag it." She put a red check by the *Nathaniel on security monitor* sighting.

"Why flag it?"

"Because your brother doesn't drink." She held his gaze. "Ever. Why is that?"

"Our dad…" His voice trailed off.

She didn't push him. "Well, he doesn't drink and I doubt he knows any card games besides Go Fish. That scene was a setup to convince you to stop looking for him."

"Which doesn't mean he's alive."

"Man, you're making this hill steeper and steeper, you know that?"

Dalton glanced at his cell phone. "Keen," he answered. "I'm not sure it matters anymore. They found my brother's body—"

"Hey!" Sydney tossed a marker at him.

"Correction, my brother's car was found on fire with a body inside. Yeah?…I don't know….I hadn't thought about it."

He eyed Sydney and she wondered who the caller was and what he'd said that made Dalton's mind engage.

She continued drawing on the time line as she listened.

"Since when? I've got a temporary e-mail." He rattled off the address. "Thanks. I'll look for it… Sure, I'll try."

He ended his call. "That was Griff. He wanted me to ask you if you knew a guy named Pete Willis from Locke."

"Nope, why?"

"He thought it might be a lead. I told him about Nate's car." He paused. "He asked how a car could burn so hot, so quickly with response teams close by."

"Exactly! They made it blow up because if his family believes he's dead, we'll be so messed up we won't be able to think straight. We'll be of no help to the Feds, or anyone investigating Locke."

"If Locke is behind this, he knows that the autopsy will reveal the truth." He paced to the window. "They must have planned the accident to buy time. Which means, something big is happening in the next few days and they're using Nate's death as a distraction."

"And after it's over, Locke will, what? Disappear?"

"Locke isn't the type to run and hide. He wouldn't sacrifice his standing or his company. If the Feds uncover something, Locke would place the blame elsewhere."

"You mean, on Nate?"

"Sure, it's perfect. When the truth comes out, Locke sets up Nate to be the prime suspect, then makes it look like Nate set up his own death, yet he's alive, living on a beach somewhere." Dalton paused. "What the hell am I talking about? We saw my brother's picture on the news. He's dead. This is ludicrous." He ran his hand down his stubbled jaw.

"No, this makes sense. Locke is waiting for Nate to finish his special project and needs to stall."

"Assuming this is true, once my brother gives them what they want, he's a dead man."

"Then we'd better find him ASAP."

"Griff's e-mailing some documentation he dug up about Locke and his bodyguards."

"Goody." She rubbed her hands together, then drew another line from Alan's name to the party.

The energy had shifted in a positive direction. Dalton

didn't act as lost as he'd been an hour ago, and actually seemed hopeful that his brother was alive and they could find him.

"Interesting," he said, eyeing the laptop.

"Share, please."

"The bald bodyguard is a former CIA double agent and one of Locke's buddies was charged with fraud last year."

"Criminals stick together, is that where you're going with this?"

"Historically speaking, yes." He closed the laptop.

"Hey, can I check my e-mail?"

"Sure." He sat at the table and slid the laptop across to her. She signed into her account and he eyed her poster board.

"What's this mark mean?" He pointed to the board.

"It's the DVD. Nathaniel borrowed it which caused me to go to his place and find you and discover that the laptop was missing."

"Why the drawing and writing down of everything?"

"It helps me make sense of things. I was taught to map things out with pictures to help me with my learning disability."

"What kind of learning disability?"

"They said dyslexia, but they call everything dyslexia. It's a brain-writing thing. I struggle with numbers, and have sequencing issues. My folks hired a tutor who taught me how to map things out so they'd make sense." She opened an e-mail from Drew Crane. It was blank.

Three more followed, then a fourth with a subject header: IMPORTANT.

It read:

Don't believe everything you see on television.

"Ah! Dalton, look at this."

He knelt beside her and read the e-mail. "What the hell? He knows something."

"And *I* know where he lives." She turned to Dalton, whose face was too darn close. "He had the team over for a boccie ball tournament," she said. Was her voice tighter than usual or was it her imagination?

One thing she didn't imagine was the tension arcing between them. Yes, to be expected. This was an intense situation revolving around life…or death.

"My orders are to stay here with you," he said, his gaze drifting to her lips.

"Your orders are to keep an eye on me." She stood and brushed past him, fighting the sexual attraction. "I'm going to Drew's. You coming?"

He stood and hesitated.

"What?" she challenged.

"I'm not at the top of my game right now, and I don't want to see you hurt."

"Drew's a friend. There's no danger there."

"Hang on a second." He planted his hands to his hips and took a deep breath, then another.

It was as if he was centering himself.

"Okay, we'll do this," he said. "But let me lead. Pack up your stuff. We'll move to another hotel tonight."

"Why?"

"Precaution."

They gathered their things and he checked out over the television.

"We should probably rent a car under one of my other names," he said, placing her shopping bag of clothes in the back of his SUV.

She placed her rolled up poster in the back next to her bag.

"Thanks," he said, slamming the truck door.

"No problem." She started for the passenger side of the car and he grabbed her wrist. She turned to him.

"I mean it, thanks." With a slight smile, his eyes warmed with gratitude.

She read the message there: he was thanking her for bringing him back from the cliff of despair and giving him hope.

"My pleasure."

Stroking her cheek with his thumb, he said, "You are something."

"A good something?" she whispered.

"A great something."

She thought he might kiss her again. She wetted her lips.

"We'd better get moving," he said.

"Okay."

They didn't move for a good five seconds. Finally, he walked her over to the passenger side of the car.

Whew, that was close. Close to a maelstrom of outrageous emotions. She wasn't sure how much longer she could control her need to touch him, to nurture the hardened soldier with a fragile soul.

They drove in contemplative silence to the University District. Drew had lived there when he attended the University of Washington and could never bring himself to leave. He loved the energy of being around college students.

"People do strange things in highly emotional situations," Dalton randomly blurted out.

"Oh, okay." What the heck was she supposed to do with that?

They turned onto Drew's street and parked down the block from the brick bungalow. Dalton pulled his firearm from the glove box and attached it to his belt.

"Stay here," he said.

"Not happening," she argued.

"Sydney—"

"Let's go." She swung open her door and started for the house.

Dalton caught up to her. "Hang on. Let me go first."

She motioned with her hand for him to lead, and she stepped into his shadow as he made his way up the steps to the front door. Rock music echoed through the windows, the bass line pounding against her chest.

She reached around him and pressed the doorbell. They waited a few minutes and she rang again. Drew didn't answer.

"The stereo's too loud," he said, peering into the front window. "I can't see anything."

"Maybe he's in the back den."

They walked down the driveway to the back porch. She hesitated when she noticed the back door cracked open.

"Dalton?"

He put his hand out to keep her behind him.

"Maybe he forgot to the close the door when he got home," she said. She hoped.

He ignored her and knocked on the door. "Drew Crane?" he called out, stepping into the kitchen.

She followed, a sick feeling settling in her stomach. Staying close to the wall, they made their way to the front room where it looked like a tornado had torn through the place. Books were scattered on the floor, furniture was flipped upside down and broken.

Her gaze stumbled onto Drew's still body lying on the floor. She grew light-headed as Dalton knelt beside her friend and checked for a pulse. Dalton glanced over his shoulder, shaking his head.

Drew was dead because he'd sent Syd an e-mail, which meant *they* knew he'd sent it to her. Which meant...

She was next.

The music pounded in her ears and the room spun so fast she couldn't get her bearings.

"Dalton," she gasped. And the darkness swallowed her.

Chapter Twelve

An hour after Dalton and Syd found Drew Crane's body they were sitting in a room in the North Precinct of the Seattle PD waiting for homicide detectives to finish up their questioning.

Dalton put his arm around Sydney and pulled her close. "Don't ever do that again," he whispered into her hair.

"What, faint?"

"Yeah. You scared the crap out of me."

"Sorry. You'd think I'd be used to seeing dead bodies by now."

"You didn't expect this one."

"I can't help but think it's my fault."

He tipped her chin to look into her eyes. "Don't say that. Drew chose to send you an e-mail."

"And now he's dead."

"It's not his fault. It's not yours. You know whose fault it is. Don't let them mess with your head."

She snuggled against his chest and he wrapped his arms around her as a protective shield. He was starting to wonder not only if he'd ever find his brother, but also how he'd keep this girl safe.

His cell vibrated. "Gotta get my phone," he said, breaking the hold. She didn't move away.

"Keen," he said.

"I ordered you to stay in the hotel room," C.O. Andrews said.

"There was a development, sir. The local news reported my brother's death in a car accident."

"I'm sorry, Keen."

"Thank you, sir. But then Ms. Trent received an e-mail questioning the identity of the body."

"Do you think he's dead?"

Dalton paused, unsure of the right answer. Was he nuts to think Nate was still alive, or just using denial to get him through the grief?

He sighed. "No, sir, I'm not sure he's dead."

Syd blinked her violet eyes at him.

"But you'll accept the possibility he was into something criminal?"

Holding Sydney's gaze, he said, "No, sir, I don't believe that, either. I can see why you'd think I'm too personally involved and you're probably right. But he is my only brother and…I know he wouldn't do anything criminal."

Thanks to Syd. She'd helped Dalton understand the kind of man Nathaniel had become.

"Agent Carter discovered evidence implicating your brother, but he also found something on a top Locke official named Stewart Pratt. Besides being ex-CIA, he has ties to a suspected terrorist cell in the Middle East. I want you to stay off his radar. Your job is to protect Ms. Trent."

"Yes, sir."

"Agent Carter will be in touch. You need to step back, Keen."

"I understand, sir."

"Make sure you do. That's all."

Dalton put the phone back in its holder.

"Was that your friend, Griff?"

"Nope. My boss."

"You're in trouble, aren't you?"

"Yep."

"Damn, I got Drew killed and you fired." She eyed him. "Drew is really dead, isn't he?"

He guided her head to his chest. "It's not your fault, sweetheart."

The door opened and Detective Rush, the lead on this homicide, sat across the table from them. Dalton figured his partner was standing on the other side of the one-way glass.

"Who's Nate?" Rush asked.

Sydney sat up. "Dalton's brother, why? Did you find him?"

"Is he missing?"

"Yes, sir," Dalton said. "He's been missing since about September 14, according to Sydney's calculations."

Rush glanced at her.

"We work together," she explained.

"How well did he know Drew Crane?"

"Drew works, worked in the Technology department at Locke, Inc."

Dalton's instincts flared. "What is it?"

Rush tapped his pen to a folder in contemplation as if he didn't know how much to share.

"Please, we need to know," Dalton pushed.

The detective leaned back in his chair. "Although we thought this was originally a case of a burglary gone bad, it seems that Drew Crane committed suicide."

"What? No, that's not possible," Syd said.

"Why not?" The detective leaned forward.

"He's not the type. He was a happy guy, good at his job, fun-loving, all that stuff."

"What led you to believe that he killed himself?" Dalton asked.

"We found a note. He mentions Nate and says, 'Didn't want to live if Nate was dead.' Drew Crane was in love with your brother. Did you know that?"

More lies to keep everyone off balance.

"It's a lie. Nate loves me," Syd blurted out.

"Syd?" Dalton said.

She eyed him. "I mean, he did love me like that, then I told him I couldn't because I didn't see him that way, then he said okay and we'd be friends, but no." She looked at the cop. "He didn't look at men like that."

"How did Drew Crane die?" Dalton asked, holding Syd's hand.

"Overdose of sedatives. We found a bottle beneath the chair next to the body. Why did he think your brother was gone?"

"There was an accident earlier," Dalton said, trying to process what Locke and his man, Pratt, were up to. "My brother's burned car was found with a body inside."

"But it's not his brother, it isn't." She shook her head, panic filling her eyes.

She probably figured if they had killed Drew with such ease then they could have certainly killed Nate.

Dalton struggled not to go there himself.

"I'm sorry," Rush said.

"You're ruling this a suicide?" Dalton asked.

"Yes, although it won't be official until after the autopsy."

"I'd like to get her home," Dalton said, motioning to Syd, who'd grown unusually quiet.

"Of course. We've got your contact information," Detective Rush said. "You're planning to stay in the area?"

"Until I find my brother, yes, sir."

Besides, it wasn't like Dalton had a job to rush back to.

After this assignment his career was up for grabs. They left the station and headed out to find a new hotel.

"Storm," Sydney said.

"It looks pretty clear to me." He eyed the sky through the front windshield.

"My cat. I need my cat, Stormie."

"We'll stop by your place and get her."

She brought her knees to her chest and hugged them. Damn, she looked so utterly broken and devastated. That must have been how he'd looked after seeing his brother's photo on the news. This compassionate girl had yanked Dalton out of his misery and flooded him with hope. It was his turn to return the favor.

They stopped by her apartment to get the cat, Dalton's instincts on red alert. A few minutes later she came out of her bedroom with a cat carrier and suitcase. She snatched some DVDs from the shelf and shoved them into the side pocket.

She wheeled the suitcase across the living room.

"What all have you got there?" he asked.

"Clothes, cosmetics, journal." She looked at him with desperate eyes. "Someone's been here."

"How do you know?"

"Things are missing. Some clothes, jewelry, perfume bottles and the external hard drive from my computer."

He hugged her. "I'm sorry, honey."

She glanced up at him. "Why take Mom's perfume bottles?"

"Let's go get you safe." He opened the apartment door.

"We'll have to get more cat litter at some point," she said, wheeling past him.

It was as if focusing on taking care of her cat kept her from being sucked deeper into the vortex of panic.

He led her to the car and reached for the carrier to put it in the backseat. She wouldn't let go.

"Okay, you hold on to Storm and I'll put the suitcase in the back," he said.

She nodded.

His boss had been clear: keep her safe and stay out of the investigation. He'd been told twice now and he didn't plan to disobey the order.

Glancing around the parking lot, he noticed a maroon sedan in the corner with someone sitting behind the wheel.

He got into the SUV and pulled out of the lot. "Anything else Storm needs besides litter?" he asked to distract her.

"A feather toy would be nice." She stuck her finger through the crisscross bars of the carrier. "It's okay, Stormie. Dalton will take good care of us."

And he would. At this point his priorities were protecting Syd and finding his brother. In that order. He trusted AW-21 agents to find Nate without Dalton's emotions muddying up the waters.

He headed back to the hotel strip, taking a few detours. He eyed the rearview mirror. The maroon sedan didn't follow them.

"Nathaniel and Drew were not lovers," she announced.

"Homophobic?"

"Not at all. I would have been happy for them. But I know it's a lie, and knowing Drew's conservative family, it will crush them. More of that, what do you call it? Collateral damage?"

"It's a temporary smoke screen. We'll clear it up soon enough."

"Collateral damage," she whispered again. "That's what I am, isn't it?"

"No, ma'am. You're a smart, generous, lovely girl and I won't let anything else happen to you. I want you to pretend you're on vacation the next few days with your handsome lover." He winked.

She shook her head and glanced out the window.

"What, I'm not handsome?"

"You're plenty handsome. Don't take this the wrong way, but I want this to be over. I was okay up until this afternoon, but after I saw Drew…I guess I'm just scared."

"I'm sorry. We'll fix it. Trust me." He handed her his cell phone. "Now, find us a hotel that takes pets."

DALTON SPENT THE NEXT two days taking care of Sydney, trying to distract her from the danger outside the hotel room walls. He'd done a pretty good job. She actually smiled by the end of day two.

It usually would have driven him nuts to be stuck inside like this, but being with Syd, taking care of her, made it okay. Strange, since he'd never spent more than twelve hours alone with someone, and then only because he was on a search-and-rescue mission.

She was making another map of the last week to intellectualize what was happening to her, when he got a call from his C.O.

"Keen," he answered.

"Status?" C.O. Andrews asked.

"Ms. Trent is safe. We haven't left the hotel room since we last spoke."

"Good. I've sent two of our men to determine if the body in the car was your brother's."

Dalton closed his eyes and took a deep breath. "Thank you, sir."

"Don't thank me. I need you to do something that will be very difficult." He paused. "I need you to hold memorial services for your brother."

Dalton sat down at the table across from Syd who scolded the cat for scratching at Syd's poster.

"Keen, can you do that?"

"Yes, sir."

"Have the girl send an e-mail with service details to Locke employees. We want everyone there. We'll have agents watching the perimeter so the girl will be safe."

"And the purpose, sir?"

"To make Locke think you believe the lie about your brother being dead so when we orchestrate the rescue he won't see it coming."

"I understand, sir."

"Agent Carter will call with instructions."

"Do you want me to send a female agent to act as your mother?" Andrew offered.

"No, sir. I'll say she was too grief-stricken to attend."

"You'll host the memorial the day after tomorrow, Friday at 1500 hours."

"Yes, sir."

"Ms. Trent needs to play along. Will she be up to it?"

"Yes, sir."

"Good. This is about more than your family, Keen. Remember that."

"Yes, sir."

Dalton glanced at Syd, who was hugging her cat. The cat didn't look happy.

He slipped his phone in the holder. "Syd?"

"Hmm?" She laid a kiss on the cat's white fur and let her go. Storm disappeared behind the curtains. "Not as dumb as I look, huh?" Syd smiled.

"What do you mean?"

"She won't be messing with my poster anymore."

"Syd, that was my boss. We need to do something and it's not going to be easy for you."

"What?"

"We need to host a memorial service for Nate."

"But he's not—"

"I'm not saying he's dead, but we need to pretend we believe he's dead. My organization wants Locke to think we've moved on and are no longer in search of my brother."

Her eyes flared. "Ooh, to keep them off balance?"

"Yes, the day after tomorrow. You'll need to send an e-mail to someone at Locke who can get the message out about the service."

"Beverly in HR is our best bet."

"At the service we should probably act like we're together, a couple."

"And I should cry a lot," she offered.

"And I'll comfort you."

"And we'll kiss." She slapped her hand to her mouth. "I can't believe I said that."

Why? It's not like he hadn't been thinking the same thing.

"Comforting kisses can't hurt," he said. "I'll hold you, stroke your back, stuff like that." He ripped his gaze from hers, afraid she'd read the true desire in his eyes. He wasn't sure how much longer he could control this need to touch her, kiss her, and make love to her.

"That's a strange look. What's wrong, is Storm climbing up your leg?" Syd sneaked a peek under the table. "Nope, no kitty there. Uh-oh, the thought of kissing me in public freaks you out?"

"Obviously I have no problem kissing you in public." He narrowed his eyes. "I'm concerned about that thing I mentioned before."

"You mean your brain fart about people doing strange things in highly emotional situations?"

"Yep."

"Nothing strange about us kissing." She shrugged and went back to her coloring.

"Sydney?"

"Yeah?"

"I don't want you to get hurt."

"Says the man who's been stabbed, sliced and emotionally gutted when he thought his brother was dead."

"I don't want you to think kisses mean more than they mean." He sounded like an idiot, but wanted to warn her against him. Dalton Keen was not a long-term relationship type of guy.

"You think a lot for a guy. Come on, help me draw." She slapped half a dozen markers in front of him.

For once in his life, he wished he were that long-term guy, a guy who didn't crave adventure and danger.

A man who could be this woman's soul mate.

Chapter Thirteen

It was a drizzly day, giving Sydney the excuse to wear a long coat and floppy rain hat. She wasn't a liar by nature and wasn't excited at the thought of looking coworkers directly in the eyes and pretending grief over Nate's passing.

Yet, she could muster up grief at the thought of what Nate suffered at the hands of these bastards. She could also cry real tears over her well-ordered life being ripped apart.

Who knew what would happen to her after they resolved this mystery? One thing for sure, she wouldn't be taking long trips thanks to Locke employee benefits. Damn.

"We're heading to the site now," he said into an earpiece. "I'm taking off the earpiece to avoid suspicion."

He removed it from his ear and placed it into the seat pocket. "Ready?" he asked, grabbing her hand.

"Sure."

He must have heard something in her voice because he smiled and stroked her cheek. "I *will* protect you."

"And who will protect you?"

He kissed her, his lips warm and soft and she found herself wanting to stay in the car and blow off the service.

He broke the kiss. "Practice," he whispered.

"Uh-huh." She smiled and he opened the door.

They got out of the car and approached the gravesite, surrounded by Locke employees. She noticed Arthur Locke standing front and center. She burst into fake tears, wanting to lay it on thick and make him uncomfortable. She knew how men hated tears.

Then again, this was the cagey bastard who'd kidnapped her friend. He probably had no feelings at all.

She leaned against Dalton for support as he nodded for the minister to proceed.

NATE WASN'T SURE WHY they'd left him alone and didn't care. Maybe it was another test. He finally had Internet access but assumed his activity was being monitored. He figured out they'd created a firewall after his e-mails to Drew bounced back.

He could send another e-mail and tell them it was meant to test the security worm he was designing for them. Yeah, that's what he'd do.

He leaned back in his chair and interlaced his hands behind his head. He'd send a message to Syd since he knew her talent for decoding. It was a developed skill to cope with her dyslexia.

But where to send his S.O.S. e-mail? He didn't want them going after her.

Someone knocked at the door.

He sat up straight.

Baldie, who Nate discovered was named Mr. Pratt, and his monster bodyguard entered the room.

"Progress?" Pratt asked.

"Slower than I'd like, sir, I'm sorry." He hadn't figured out the disable code yet and until he did, he wasn't giving them a way into the U.S. government's mainframe. "I think you need a faster Internet provider. But I've got the basics figured out. By tomorrow evening you should be settled into the system."

"Very good, Jonas," he said, patting him on the shoulder. "How about you shoot for eight o'clock? I find it's always good to have a deadline."

Which meant if he missed it, he'd be punished.

"I'm sorry to have to give you bad news," Pratt said. "Your friend, Drew Crane, died today."

"What?" They might as well have slugged him in the chest with a steel bar.

"What happened?" Dread burned its way up his chest.

"They say it was suicide." Pratt glanced at the big guy and back to Nathaniel. "He couldn't go on living after he heard about your death."

Drew did not kill himself. These bastards killed him. Why? Because Nate had sent him an e-mail?

"Oh, and I thought you'd like to see this." Pratt placed a DVD into the laptop. "Your memorial service from earlier today. It's comforting to know how many people cared about you. Let's watch it together."

Sure, made sense. Pratt wanted to study Nate's reaction to the DVD. Nate beat back any and all emotion. It was getting easier every time.

Pratt double-clicked on the DVD icon and hit Play. As Nate watched the group of people gathered at the gravesite, he realized Pratt was letting him know that that part of Nate's life was over. He was being mourned and forgotten.

At the center of the group was his brother with a comforting arm around Sydney. She wept, Dalton hugged her, and Nate's gut twisted.

"No offense, sir, but I have work to do." He wasn't sure how much more of this he could stand. His brother and his friend were riddled with grief, yet they shouldn't be, at least not yet.

"Of course," Pratt said, and pointed to the screen. "They make a nice couple, don't you think?"

Nate shrugged.

"Your brother will be leaving shortly and Sydney's job in the IT department is going to be eliminated." He paused. "Maybe we could relocate her at the compound as your assistant?"

No, not here, don't bring her to this hell.

Pratt studied Nate's reaction.

"She is very organized, sir," Nate said, realizing this was yet another test.

"And very attractive." Pratt winked. "Look at that sweet face."

The camera zoomed in on Sydney looking up into Dalton's eyes. Nate dug his fingernails into his palm. She was in love with him. Between Nate and his brother, they were going to get her killed.

Nate couldn't let that happen. It didn't matter that she'd shunned his love and went for his brother, she'd always be his best friend. Nate couldn't allow her to be killed.

"I'll let you know if she accepts our offer to come work at the compound," Pratt said.

Accepts his offer? Like she'd have a choice? They left Nate alone, locking the dead bolt from the outside.

"Think, think." He needed to nail this program and let them peek inside long enough to think they had control, then strip the control, while leading the Feds back to the source: Locke, Inc.

He could pretend to his captors that he didn't care about Sydney, but he couldn't lie to himself. She'd done nothing to deserve being hurt by these people. And if his brother was too dense to see that she was next on their list of victims, Nate would have to save her himself. Yet he needed her help in order to save them both.

"Damn it." How could he get her a message without putting her in danger?

Not only did he have to send her a coded message, but he'd have to send it from a coded e-mail. Either that, or…

"That's it." He typed in the domain address for the Warlords of the Universe website. Syd knew it was one of Nate's favorites and the violent story line mirrored his captivity at present.

"Come on," he whispered, wishing the system was faster. It was slow because everything he did was being filtered to monitor his activity.

Fine, they'd watch him sign on to the Warlords website and write it off to his immaturity. They wouldn't realize he was trying to get Syd's attention. It was a long shot, but he had to try.

"I'm counting on you, Syd."

EVEN THOUGH IT WAS A fake service, Dalton still felt gutted. He had to act the part of grieving brother, shaking hands, accepting sympathies and consoling Sydney.

The entire time the Locke bastards stood there with long faces, acting as if they felt sorrow when in reality they seemed smug and victorious. They thought they'd gotten away with taking his little brother and using him against his country.

Dalton would find his brother, rescue him and destroy Locke for what he'd done to Nate. And Sydney.

They returned to the hotel after switching cars three times with other agents in order to keep their location from the enemy.

Dalton ripped off his suit coat and tossed it to the bed. "I'm spent."

"Me, too." Syd wrapped her arms around his chest from behind and rested her head against his back.

He could get used to this.

"But it's worth it if it helps nail the bad guys," she said.

"I can't help but think…I'll be doing this again in a month, for real."

She turned him to face her. "Don't go there, hear me? Hope is the only thing that keeps us functioning on days like this. I know, I clung to it for months before my parents died."

"But in the end, you had to accept the reality of death."

"There's no reason to accept Nathaniel's death," she said. Gripping his shoulders, she gave him a shake. "We're going to see those bright blue eyes again, and hear that ridiculous laugh and…" Her voice trailed off.

Dalton realized he'd pushed her too hard, pushed her into feeling the anguish of losing her friend.

"I'm sorry." He pulled her to his chest and held on. Damn, he wished this wasn't an illusion created by danger and violence. He wished that this woman was real and their relationship could last past the gruesome end of burying his kid brother.

"Stop it," her muffled voice said against his chest.

"What?" He tipped her chin up to look into her eyes.

"I can feel you going to that dark place and I hate it there, so stop it."

"You're right, sweetheart. You're so right."

Someone knocked on the door. Dalton motioned for her to get into the bathroom and he pulled out his firearm.

Dalton eyed the peephole and spotted Zack Carter standing outside his door.

He let the agent in.

"It's okay, Sydney," Dalton called out.

She stepped out of the bathroom.

"Agent Carter, this is Sydney Trent."

"Hi," she said, shaking his hand.

Carter motioned for them to sit. "I thought the services went well. You two were very convincing."

Dalton recognized the disapproval in the agent's tone. Not

only were Dalton and Syd convincing in their grief, but they were also convincing in their love for each other. Wasn't that the objective?

"Andrews sent me to make sure you stay out of trouble," Carter said.

"Hey, the trouble isn't his fault," Syd defended Dalton.

Dalton glanced at the floor. It was obvious she felt protective of him.

"Be that as it may, Andrews doesn't want to rush this and lose our advantage," Carter said.

"Seems like Locke's team has the advantage," Dalton challenged.

"We want it to seem that way, Keen. Look, I have some news but I don't want you to get your hopes up. The accident victim was definitely not your brother."

A squeal escaped Sydney's lips and she threw her arms around Dalton. "I told you, I told you."

Dalton kept his gaze trained on his fellow agent. "But that doesn't mean he's alive."

Carter didn't answer.

Sydney sat back and shoved at his shoulder. "Why can't you be happy? This is good news. Jerk."

"She's a civilian. She doesn't understand how this works," Dalton said.

"Don't talk about me like I'm invisible." She glared at Dalton. "I'm right here and I heard him say Nathaniel was not the dead body in the car."

"There's more," Carter said.

Dalton held his breath. It was coming, the news that they had found evidence of his brother's death in another location.

"Go on," Dalton said.

Sydney held Dalton's hand while a ball of dread formed in his throat.

"Drew Crane received an e-mail yesterday morning that we suspect was from your brother."

"Fantastic!" Syd squeezed his hand. "Did you hear that?"

"What did it say?" Dalton pushed.

"That he was on assignment in China and to tell Sydney," he said as he looked at Syd, "that she'd find the DVD next to the hamster cage."

"He doesn't have a hamster," she said.

"You think it was legit?" Dalton asked.

"Not sure." Carter crossed his arms over his chest. "The e-mail was recalled by the source, which was a maze of IP addresses so we couldn't locate the origin. Drew Crane spent an hour tracking it and opened the file."

"Which is what got him killed," Dalton hushed.

"Looks that way. I need to know," he said and then paused, "if you think there was anything to the rumor about them being romantically involved." He directed the question at Sydney.

"No. They were friends, and Drew had a long-time girl-friend. I think I would have sensed something."

"Were you and Nate lovers?" Carter asked.

"Too personal, bub."

"What's next?" Dalton asked, trying to derail this line of questioning. Although she'd repeatedly denied a romantic in-volvement with Nate, the thought still taunted Dalton.

"We wait a few days for Locke's men to lower their guard."

"I'm afraid they've made my brother do something against his country," Dalton said. "I'm not sure we have the luxury of time."

"We'll actively work on finding the source of the e-mail and tracking your brother. But we need you two to act like you've given up and moved on. I'll be close if you need me. Andrews would prefer you stay in the hotel room."

"Yes, sir," Dalton said, walking him to the door. "Thanks for the update."

Carter left and Dalton shut and double-locked the door.

"Isn't that great?" Sydney said, launching herself into his arms. He held on for a second, then let go and set her safely aside.

"What's wrong?" she asked.

"It doesn't mean he's alive."

"Oh, for Pete's sake, enjoy the moment, nurture the hope that's buried in there." She grabbed his shirt and tugged as if trying to find the hope hidden in his chest.

Then she looked up and smiled.

And kissed him.

She tasted of honey and sunshine and he fought back the urge to take her right there. After all, she was his brother's girl, right? She'd slept with Nate.

He broke the kiss. "We can't do this, Syd."

She looked up at him. "Why not? Come on, Dalton, you know there's something between us and I don't mean that whole people-do-strange-things-in-intense-situations line. You can make up excuses all you want, but this is real and it feels right and—"

"You slept with my brother."

She stepped back as if he'd slapped her. "No, I didn't."

"You wouldn't answer Carter when he asked you flat out."

She planted her hands to her hips. "It's none of his business."

"But it's mine. He's my brother."

"Nate's my best friend. That doesn't mean we slept together."

"Then why didn't you admit as much to Carter?"

"Because it's embarrassing, okay? The fact is I've only been with one guy and it was a stupid high school thing and

I've never slept with another man because I've been busy and didn't have time to date and then when I finally started dating, I felt insecure and scared. I didn't know what I was doing and I was afraid…oh, never mind."

She shoved a few pillows against the headboard of the bed, grabbed the remote and turned on the TV.

"What were you afraid of?" Dalton asked.

"This conversation was over five minutes ago," she said, staring at the screen.

He sat beside her and took the remote from her hand. Turning off the TV, he looked at her. "What were you afraid of?"

"Being laughed at because of my inexperience. Giving myself to someone who wouldn't appreciate it. Giving myself to the wrong person just to feel like an experienced woman. There, confessions by Sydney Trent over. Give me the remote."

"I'm sorry I pushed. But I thought—"

"What, if I had slept with your brother I couldn't sleep with you? Yeah, I know, I'm such a sweet girl, right?"

"No, this is about me. I've failed my brother over and over and I didn't want to take the one thing that mattered to him, even if he was dead."

"But I'm not his, and he's not dead. Didn't you hear Agent Carter? If that isn't a strong case for hope I don't know what is. Hope, Dalton, feel it."

She looked at him with those violet eyes tinted with promise and his armor cracked.

"Only do it if you want to," she said, reading his mind.

"You have no idea how much I want to."

"I think I do." She lay back on the bed and tugged on his hand until he lay beside her.

As they lay side by side he wasn't sure how to do this, how to make love to this gentle woman without hurting her, physically or emotionally.

"Sydney—"

"Shh." She pressed her forefinger to his lips. "This is right. It has nothing to do with your brother, or the danger we're in making us do strange things. It's about two people who want each other." She glanced at his lips and offered a slight smile. "And I've never been this bold before in my life." She glanced into his eyes. "The only reason I can be this bold is because it's you. You're the man I want. Please tell me I'm not making a complete fool of myself."

He framed her cheek with his hand. She closed her eyes and leaned into his touch.

"You're not a fool. You're a sweet girl."

"But do you want to make love to me?" she whispered. Her breath warmed his palm.

"Yes," he said.

She turned her cheek and pressed kisses against his palm. His body lit with need as her warm, moist tongue flirted with his hand, shooting shock waves of desire up his arm and across his shoulders.

"Syd, you are so beautiful," he whispered, trailing his hand behind her head and pulling her forward to get a taste of her honey-sweet lips.

She moaned as she deepened the kiss and he thought he'd lose it right there. But he couldn't. He wanted her to feel treasured and…loved, even if he feared he was incapable of the emotion.

He'd taken women quickly in the past, without thought or promise. Not this girl. They might split apart once Nate was found, but he wanted to pleasure her tonight in ways that would bind her to him forever. Even when she found her life mate, the man who'd travel with her, laugh with her and father her children, she'd remember this night in Dalton's arms.

This woman had given him so much. She'd awakened his sense of humor, challenged his cynicism and taught him to hope. He realized that he'd never felt hope before, not growing up, and certainly not being assigned to gruesome missions.

He'd created a shell of protection around his soul to cope with his life. This sweet girl had pierced it, letting in the light.

He wanted more, more of her spark and energy. He needed to be a part of her, to be inside of her.

She broke the kiss, rolled him onto his back and climbed on top. She unbuttoned his shirt, pulled it from his pants and eased her hands beneath his undershirt, trailing her fingertips up and across his chest.

"Sydney," he moaned, closing his eyes.

"Get all these clothes off," she said. She slipped his shirts up and over his head, leaving him naked from the waist up.

With warm, wanting lips, she layered kisses against his chest, whispering promises against his skin.

His hands tightened on her hips, as he struggled to keep it under control. He wasn't used to a woman taking the lead, wasn't used to lying back and letting someone pleasure him like this.

He fingered the hem of her skirt, inching his hands up her thighs, and tugged her panties down to stroke the warmth between her legs.

"Dalton," she gasped, gripping his chest and arching her back.

"What do you want, sweetheart?"

"I want our clothes off," she said with wicked smile.

"Done." He pulled her blouse and camisole up and over her head to reveal a white lace bra. Her nipples pierced the delicate fabric. He ached to taste them, but first he needed to undress her completely.

He unclasped her bra, freeing beautiful, wanting breasts. He unzipped her skirt and skimmed his thumbs beneath the waistband and panties. In a second they were down and he rolled her onto her back to completely rid her of clothing. She lay there, breathing heavy, wanting him.

"Kiss me," she said.

"Where? Here?" He leaned forward and kissed her breast. Once. Twice, a third time, all the while unbuckling his pants and shucking them and his boxers. There was nothing between them now, not a shred of fabric, not his brother, not even the danger threatening their lives.

There was just Syd and Dalton, two adults about to share the most treasured gift between a man and woman.

"Or here?" he said, layering kisses down to her belly button, while stroking her nipple with his thumb.

"I'm going to explode," she hissed.

"I want to see that," he whispered, planting a kiss between her legs.

She dug her fingernails into his back and arched for him. "Up here, I need you up here, kissing me."

He layered kisses all the way up her rib cage to her breast and laved her nipple. Its taste would be burned into his psyche forever.

It was perfect. She was perfect. This wasn't a quickie, or a game to slake his lust.

"Inside of me." She wrapped her arm around his backside and squeezed his butt.

"Is that an order?"

"Yes, soldier. On top of me and inside of me." Her violet eyes widened with need. "Now."

"I've got a better idea."

"Better?"

He rolled onto his back, slipped on a condom and encouraged her to straddle him. She slipped so comfortably into place. He cupped her breasts, teasing the hard points, wanting to see her face as she exploded into nirvana.

"Dalton," she whispered.

"You're so beautiful," he said, one hand teasing her nipple, while he slipped the other between their bodies in search of the spot that would set her off.

She arched, taking him fully inside of her. He wasn't sure how long he could hold back. His body ached to fill her with his love, ached for a genuine connection to this woman.

She leaned forward and kissed him, a hard, demanding kiss, then arched again, opening wider and taking him deeply to the point where he found himself completely lost.

Yet he was right where he belonged: in the arms and body of the woman he loved.

"Dalton," she whispered, with desperation.

"Let go, my love."

She arched one last time and let out a cry of pleasure that set off his release inside of her. Mind-blowing stars shattered across the backs of his eyelids. Didn't know sex could feel like this. But then again, for the first time, this wasn't *just* sex.

She collapsed against him. "So, that's what making love feels like?"

"Yeah," he said. It both thrilled and terrified him.

"Amazing," she whispered and snuggled against his chest.

That was one word for it. He didn't want to think of other words, didn't want to be pulled back into his cynical self. Dalton Keen wanted to spend the next few hours holding the woman he loved, ignoring the realities of life, and pretending he could live happily ever after.

Even if he knew it was a lie.

Chapter Fourteen

How could something so wonderful be so scary? Sydney stroked her lover's naked chest and closed her eyes.

They'd made love not once, but twice, and both times she'd nearly cried. But she'd held back, not wanting to frighten him. He wouldn't understand. Her tears were those of a woman in love, a woman who'd experienced something so utterly precious, something she secretly feared she'd never find.

No, with her learning disability making her different growing up, then having to take care of her parents, she'd never had much time to develop an easiness with men.

Uh, bad choice of words, Syd.

What did it mean to have this man in her bed? Was this a one-time deal for him? A great screw to hold him until his next assignment?

God, please don't let this be a one-nighter.

"You okay?" he asked, stroking her hair.

Holy cats, he'd read her mind?

"Yeah, very much okay." She balanced her chin on an upturned palm to study him. "You?"

"Pretty damn okay." He shot her a smile and she caught sight of that dimple again, the one that made him look so young and hopeful.

"You seem better today," she teased.

"Nothing like a good night's sleep to—"

She whacked him in the shoulder. "Jerk."

"Yeah, well." He eyed her. "I'm not good at the mushy stuff."

"What if you *were* good at the mushy stuff? What would you say?" she asked. This was it. His response would give her an inkling of whether or not she was a one-time fling.

"I guess I'd say that last night was the most incredible night of my life. Sounds cliché."

"Keep going."

"That I'd like to promise more nights like that but," he said as he pinned her with intense aquamarine eyes, "I can't think about the future, or make promises until I've found my brother. I need resolution there." He paused. "One way or the other."

She sighed with relief. Okay, he wasn't calling her a one-night stand. A good sign.

"There is only one resolution, love," she said. "We're going to find him, alive. But we can't do it lying here, can we?"

She jumped out of bed and marched to the bathroom.

"Nice ass," he called after her.

"Fire up the laptop. We've got work to do."

She shut the door and eyed her naked reflection in the mirror. Had she really paraded herself in complete nakedness in front of him? Sure, why not? He'd seen it all; touched it all…kissed it all.

Her legs went wobbly and she figured she'd better get a grip, maybe with help from a cold shower, if she was going to try and track down Nate.

The thought had come to her early this morning, in the semi-conscious hours between sleep and wakefulness. Those were always her best times, the times when inspiration hit like a door opening into a colorful garden.

And the inspiration whispered: *Find him, Syd. You're the only one who can find Nathaniel.*

True. She knew him better than anyone, yet she'd been so wrapped up in trying to stay safe this past week she hadn't had a lot of time to go digging.

Well, now she had tons of time, time in a hotel room with Dalton. They could pass the time in each other's arms, but that wouldn't help her get any closer to her end goal: loving Dalton for the rest of his life.

"Oh, girl, you are in trouble," she whispered to her reflection. She'd fallen fast and hard for the guy and all she could get from him was the comment that he couldn't think about the future until he'd found Nathaniel.

And then?

"And then you live happily ever after," she whispered.

She deserved happiness and so did Dalton. They'd battled their share of grief and devastation, and in this situation they would work together to prevent another devastation from destroying them.

They'd find his brother.

"Get to work, girl."

After a quick, cool shower she came out of the bathroom wrapped in a towel.

"Have fun?" he asked from his prone position in bed.

"Hey, lazy butt, get up and get me some food. I need brain energy to get started."

"Started on what?"

"I'm going to find your brother and you're going to help me."

"But—"

"Now, soldier!"

"I'm not sure I like your bossy side."

She ambled to the bed and planted a kiss on his lips. "Better?"

"Yeah." He reached for her towel and she slapped his hand.

"Down, boy. Food, then research, *then* playtime."

"Promise?"

"Yep."

At the promise of playtime Dalton sprung from the bed, dressed and went in search of food. Syd got dressed in jeans and a sweatshirt, and considered possible e-mail accounts Nate might use to send an S.O.S. She knew Nate had a few anonymous online identities, but when she checked them she came up empty.

Dalton returned with a bag of groceries and more poster board. "Some guys bring roses. I bring poster board."

"How thoughtful." She kissed him and placed the white board on the table. "You can help me with this. We need to start by pretending we're Nathaniel." She grabbed an apple from the bag of groceries and paced to the door and back. "You're Nathaniel and you've been tricked into doing something immoral."

"Illegal."

"The illegal part wouldn't bother him as much as the immoral part. You've figured out you've been used to do something immoral, but they catch you and lock you up."

"We don't know they—"

"Play along." She bit into the apple and chewed, narrowing her eyes. "You're locked up. Can't get away, but they want something from you, so you use that to your advantage."

"Unless they've broken you already."

She threw her apple, nailing him in the chest.

"Hey! You sure you don't moonlight for the Mariners?" he said with a mock-pained expression.

"Stop with the negative stuff. You're Nathaniel, which means you're as smart as Einstein—"

"Actually, his IQ is higher than Einstein's—"

"You're smarter than Einstein, you've been kidnapped to work on a special, immoral project and you need help to escape. He e-mailed Drew, so Nate must have access to the Internet."

"And Drew's dead."

"If Nathaniel knows that, he won't use direct e-mail again for fear of getting someone else killed."

"That wasn't his fault."

"You and I know that, but Nathaniel will shoulder that guilt. Kind of like how you blame yourself for Nate being sucked into this."

"Guess it's a family weakness."

She stepped up to him and kissed his cheek. "More like a family strength. So, you can't send an e-mail, but you need to contact someone for help. If his Internet activity is being monitored, he'd have to leave the S.O.S. where the bad guys wouldn't recognize it as significant."

Sitting at the computer, she began her search of Internet sites Nathaniel frequented.

Dalton touched her shoulder. "Thanks."

"Hey, it's completely selfish. I want this over to get my life back." *And get you in my bed.*

She checked a few sites but nothing unusual popped up.

"Come on, Nathaniel. I know you're out there. Talk to me."

She checked five more. Nothing.

"You need to draw?" Dalton offered, biting into a sandwich.

"Not now, not now."

She nibbled her thumbnail and tried another site, the Warlords of the Universe site. It wasn't one of her favorites since it had a little too much torture and death for her taste.

Torture and death. Exactly what Nathaniel was going through if their theory was right and Locke baddies had kidnapped him.

The hair bristled on the back of her neck. "Of course."

She signed on to her Warlords account but a message popped up blocking her from entering the site.

"What the heck is this about?"

She tried again. No dice.

Finding the customer service link, she went into a chat room to find help.

"Video games," Dalton muttered.

Syd wasn't thwarted. She kept asking how to reactivate her account. Finally, half an hour later, a service rep sent her an IM indicating that she'd been accused of breaking into an account and stealing points.

She held her breath. Typed in the question:

Who accused me of stealing?

Waited. Took a deep breath.
And the answer popped up:

Wizard X.

"Yes!" she cried, jumping to her feet.

"What, did you beat the dragon master or something?"

"It's him! It's Nate. He's locked me out to get my attention."

Dalton stood, slowly, and looked at the screen. "How do you know that?"

"Because the player who blocked me is Wizard X. That's Nathaniel's name in Warlords of the U. He's alive, Dalton. He's alive and trying to send us a message."

AN HOUR LATER AW-21 had assigned their best techs to figure out Nate's message buried in Syd's online gaming account.

"He's really alive?" Dalton asked.

"And we're going to find him," Sydney said, clapping her hands.

A knock interrupted their celebration. She automatically went into the bathroom and Dalton went to the door, once again spotting Agent Carter in the hallway. He let him in.

"Come on out, Syd," he said and turned to Carter. "What's up?"

"Gotta move you, both of you. That account we accessed for Ms. Trent was tagged which means they're trying to figure out where you are."

"Can they do that?" Sydney asked, shoving her things into the backpack. She peeked behind the curtains and snatched the cat from her hiding place.

"Can't risk it. Let's move."

Dalton could care less about his things. He had to protect Syd. "Where to?"

"Safe house."

They rushed down the hallway to the parking lot and got into Zack Carter's SUV. They headed north. "Our techs thought they found something, but it turns out it's gibberish," Carter said. "Our guys are trying to make sense of it, but aren't having any luck."

"Let me see it," Syd said from the backseat.

"Don't be offended, miss, but if our government experts can't make sense of it, I'm not sure—"

"You've got nothing to lose. Let me have a crack at it."

Carter looked to Dalton for help.

"She and my brother are best friends," Dalton said. "Maybe something will make sense to her because of their connection."

"When we get to the safe house, I'll find you a hard copy."

Fifteen minutes later they pulled up to an apartment

complex on the other side of town. Agent Carter escorted Dalton and Sydney inside a nicely furnished apartment. Carter signed on to his computer and printed out a copy of the code they'd found on the Warlords website.

"Get me my poster board and markers," Syd said.

Dalton shrugged at his fellow agent and did as she asked. But two hours later she still hadn't made sense of it.

"Syd, honey, it's okay if you can't figure it out," Dalton said, rubbing her shoulders.

She acted as if she didn't hear him or feel him touching her.

Carter stood guard at the window overlooking the parking lot.

"Holy crap!" she cried, pointing at her poster board. "Way to go, Nathaniel!"

It looked like a bunch of nonsense to Dalton.

"What's she talking about?" Carter said from his post.

"It's all right here. Look." She held up the poster board as if displaying a product for purchase. "Every fourth letter makes a word, because his birthday is the fourth month, April. So here's what I've got:

Being held at Locke cp. Security breach in 24. Check XM.

"XM? The DVD!" She raced to her suitcase and dug through the contents, pulling out the *X-Men* DVD Nate had borrowed. She opened it and found what looked like a blank CD. "It's not the movie, but I'll bet it's better." She handed it to Carter. "My guess is it's evidence against Locke."

"They forced Nate to breach the security system," Dalton said, pacing. "Hell, once they get in, his life is over."

"You've got to save him," Sydney said to Carter.

Carter popped the CD into his laptop and scanned the files. "Damn good evidence against Locke and his people."

"Can you arrest them?" Syd asked.

"No time for that," Dalton said. "The security breach is happening two hours from now. I've got to save my brother."

"Yes, we do." Carter e-mailed information from the CD to Washington, D.C. "We could use his help to interpret all this information. I'll call Andrews." He pulled out his cell phone.

Dalton hugged Sydney. "You didn't tell me you're so damn smart."

"Sometimes the answers are right in front of you."

Yeah, like this answer. Like the fact he loved this woman and not just because she might have saved his brother's life, and the country from disaster. He loved her for her hope and determination, for her sense of humor and because, well, because she was Syd.

"We've got approval to go in," Carter said. "I've got to get a team together."

Dalton walked him to the door. "Listen, Carter—"

"I know what you're going to ask." He glanced over Dalton's shoulder at Syd, who was sweet-talking the cat. "Someone needs to watch the girl, you know that."

"We'll set her up with the lookout," Dalton said. "She'll be safe."

He nodded. "Be ready in ninety minutes."

"Thank you, sir."

"Officially, I told you no."

"Yes, sir."

Carter left and Dalton locked the door.

"What happens now?" she asked.

"I go with them to rescue Nate."

She stood and the cat jumped from her arms. "No."

"No?"

"You could be hurt."

"That's my job."

"Okay, I get that but, oh, fiddle fudge." She interlaced her fingers and squeezed her hands together. "I just found you and we get along really well and you understand me and you don't make fun of my poster drawings and—"

He hugged her. "I need to be there for my brother." He broke the embrace and looked into her eyes. "I don't know what they've done to him, Syd. I need to be there when they pull him out of that hell. Do you understand, honey?"

"Yeah, I wish I didn't. I wish I could convince you not to leave me."

"Who said I was leaving you?"

THE GLOWING DIGITAL numbers of the clock taunted Nate as he struggled to focus. It was closing in on six and he still didn't have the shut down code figured out. Damn, he'd have to give them something, right?

A woman's scream echoed through the door. He pushed away from the desk and pressed his ear against the door to listen.

"Help me!" a woman cried.

"Sydney?"

"No, don't touch me!" she screamed. "Nathaniel!"

"Sydney!" He pounded on the door.

"Help! Don't…help me!" the voice grew farther away.

"Syd!" he cried.

The door unlocked and he stepped back breathing heavy through clenched teeth.

Mr. Pratt entered the room, followed by a man Nate had never seen before. A tall, slim man.

"I have good news for you, Jonas," Pratt said. "Sydney Trent has agreed to join our team."

"That, that was her?"

Pratt smiled.

"She didn't sound like she agreed."

Meat Mallet bodyguard stepped into the room, massaging his fist as if he'd just hit something.

Nate was going to be sick. He stumbled back against the desk.

"Why Jonas, you said you didn't care about Sydney since she's with your brother. Were you lying to us?"

He glanced from Pratt to the stranger, to Meat Mallet Man.

"I don't like to see anybody hurt. It's my nature."

"Here I'd thought we'd changed your nature." Pratt nodded and the stranger came up behind him. "Now, Jonas, you lied about your feelings for Ms. Trent. I'd hate to think you lied about the INXP project."

"No sir, I didn't lie."

Lock down your feelings. Don't let these bastards get to you. You need to save Sydney.

The skinny stranger pulled Nate's arms behind his back in an arm lock.

Meat Mallet Man came around and let one fly, nailing Nate in the gut. He coughed, started to go down, but the stranger held him steady. Another blow, another cracked rib, and all he could think about was that this same fist had hit Sydney.

Nate could hardly breathe after the third blow.

The stranger released him and Nate fell to the floor. Pratt slapped Nate's cheeks and he opened his eyes.

"You have two hours. Mr. Locke expects results. If we're not up and running in two hours, killing Ms. Trent will be the kindest thing we do to her."

Nate closed his eyes. This must have been his last, final test of loyalty. And he'd failed, miserably.

"On the other hand, if you provide us with a way into the security system, we will hand her over to you relatively unharmed." He stood. "Fair enough?"

The men left Nate lying on the floor, curled into a helpless ball once again. He hated himself, loathed Nathaniel Keen, the dorky, computer geek who couldn't defend himself or save his sweet friend, Sydney. And where the hell was Dalton?

He'd given up on Nate, that's where he was. Back in the field somewhere, stalking, shooting, rescuing.

And somehow, he wasn't sure how, Nate had to protect his country and save Sydney.

Chapter Fifteen

At seven fifty-two, Nate tested the program and fought back the bile rising in his throat.

He'd done it. He'd effectively created a portal into the United States Government's secure mainframe, allowing these bastards to access top secret information so they could present themselves as the heroes when they provided the only program that would defend against the breach.

For tonight, Nate had set it up so they'd be able to access information for a limited amount of time, fifteen minutes. Then it would shut down, and in those precious fifteen minutes, Homeland Security would be alerted to the breach in the system and Nate would be down the hall saving Sydney. He'd figured out how to disengage the Locke compound security system, how to set off alarms, and lock doors that shouldn't be locked and open doors that should be.

He hit the intercom.

"Yes, Jonas?" Pratt answered.

"I've finished, sir. And we're in."

Nate stared at the screen, calming his heartbeat, readying himself to grab Sydney and race the hell out of there. Where would they go? He hadn't a clue. Dalton was probably long gone.

The click of the lock unnerved him. *Focus. Don't lose it now.*

"Jonas, show us your work," Pratt said, coming up behind him.

"What about Sydney?"

"You get us in and we'll give you the key to her room."

Meat Mallet Man waved a keycard in Nate's face. Nate focused on the screen. "It's simple. I've designed code to get us in without being noticed," he lied. He opened the program, typed in his password and the Great Seal of the United States appeared on the screen.

"Fantastic," Pratt said in awe. He motioned for Nate to move aside and Nate stood.

Nate had fifteen minutes and counting.

Pratt clicked on a folder icon for the CIA and it opened to reveal a list of agent names. "Outstanding." He looked at Nate. "We've started a pre-celebration downstairs. Go get yourself a glass of champagne."

Nate hesitated.

"Jonas?" Pratt questioned him.

"I'd like to see Sydney now."

"So you would." Pratt waved him off and Meat Mallet Man held up the keycard. "You want this? Come get it." Nate hesitated and the guy burst out laughing and tossed it on the floor.

Nate scrambled to pick up the card and raced down the hall. He wasn't sure which room she was in, which room the keycard opened. He tried two, three, and on the fourth room, he heard the click and whipped open the door.

"Syd, I'm here." He froze at the sight of a disheveled, empty bed and handcuffs dangling from the metal frame.

"Syd?" He scanned the room, spotted her mother's perfume bottles and jewelry box on the dresser. Next to the box was a photograph of Syd and Nate taken at the Space Needle.

But where was Syd? He searched the attached bathroom, whipped open the closet, looked behind a love seat, then his eyes caught on a cream colored blouse balled up on the floor…spotted with blood.

"Things got a little out of hand last night," Meat Mallet Man said from the doorway.

Rage clawed its way up Nate's chest. "No!" He charged the bastard.

The guy grabbed the desk chair and swung, nailing Nate in the stomach. He fell to his knees.

Sydney.

Dead.

She'd been here, so close. And Nate had been too late.

"When will you get it?" Meat Mallet Man said. "You've got to stop picking on guys bigger than you." He squeezed Nate's jaw between his iron fingers. "Oh, right, everyone's bigger than you. And stronger."

The bully left, locking Nate inside the room where they'd killed Syd.

Beside Nate on the floor was the bloodstained, white blouse, the one she'd worn when they went for Italian and she wouldn't eat because she was afraid she'd spill red sauce on herself.

Gripping the blouse between his fingers, he inhaled her sweet scent.

"Sydney," he cried her name into the soft fabric, sullied with blood.

There was no point in fighting anymore. The bastards had won.

And in fifteen minutes they'd come looking for him, force him to fix the bug that kicked them out of the government's secure system.

Unless he destroyed them all. He glanced across the room

and spotted a bottle of hand sanitizer on a small, white cabinet. Yes, he'd cleanse himself; cleanse all of them...

With fire.

DALTON KNEW HE WAS AN unofficial guest on this mission and respected his role. He'd set up Sydney up with the lookout agent at Carillon Heights Apartments which had an extensive view of the waterfront. She had infrared binoculars to keep watch of what was going on.

On the boat with Dalton was lead Agent Carter, and Agent Munno.

"Cougar One to Cougar Two, over," Carter said into his handheld radio.

"Read you, Cougar One, over," the lookout responded.

"We're about two hundred meters out, over."

Carter glanced at Dalton and shook his head. "I could get in deep for bringing you along."

"I do appreciate it, sir."

"Yeah, yeah." He held the radio to his mouth. "Cougar Two, what's your visual?"

"A lot of activity, sir. Seems to be a party on the back deck, over."

"Damn, they're not going to make this easy," Carter said to himself.

"Cougar One, there's been a complication. Emergency vehicles are headed for the residence, over."

"Dalton, the house is on fire," Syd cried through the radio.

NATE SAT AGAINST THE wall, barely feeling the heat. It was right that it should end this way, that he should die holding Syd's blouse in his hands.

The door swung open and someone grabbed him by the shoulders. His vision blurred.

"He's on fire," a voice said.

"Get him to the boat," another ordered.

Nate struggled to think. *No, don't struggle. You've fought your whole life: for love, for self-respect. Let it go.*

He was hoisted over someone's shoulder like a sack of rice. They needed his genius to get back into the system.

They'd never let him go.

Alarms echoed in his head, screams, cries for help. He would have cried out, but his voice was paralyzed, frozen in his chest. Everything frozen and numb.

He closed his eyes, surrendering whatever fight he had left in him.

The only thing worth fighting for had been Sydney. Now she was gone, Nate was officially dead, and he'd betrayed his country.

There was no reason to fight anymore. No reason to live.

"GET CLOSER," DALTON ordered, stepping up to the side of the boat.

Carter glared at him in warning.

"Let me help," Dalton said.

"Cougar Two to Cougar One, two boats are pulling away from a boathouse on the south side of the property, over."

Dalton grabbed the radio from Carter. "Syd, do you see Nate?"

"I think…hang on…I see him on the second boat with the white and green lights," she said.

Carter snatched the radio back. "Cougar Two, I need position on response teams, over."

"Kirkland Fire Department, and I see a King County Marine Rescue boat, over."

"I see Nate," Syd said. "He's standing up…he looks confused."

"Get closer," Dalton said, then eyed Carter. "Sorry."

"Closer," Carter ordered Agent Munno.

"No, Nate! Dalton, Nate went overboard," Syd cried.

Dalton ripped off his jacket and sweater, and grabbed a wet suit. He knew this might happen, was ready for it. He glanced at Carter.

"Go," Carter ordered.

Dalton jumped into the frigid water and fought the shock to his system. He had a wet suit on and his brother didn't, which meant he'd freeze, and his street clothes would drag him down.

The King County Rescue boat aimed a spotlight at the water and Dalton caught sight of his brother's head bobbing above the surface. Dalton swam toward him and grabbed Nate by the collar. A sob racked Dalton's chest.

He got Nate to the boat and handed him off to Carter.

"Man overboard," Carter shouted.

Dalton glanced over his shoulder and spotted Locke's bald bodyguard trying to escape by swimming to shore.

"Not on your life, buddy." Dalton went after the guy, grabbed him and dragged him to the boat.

Carter and Munno pulled him up as Dalton took a few breaths and watched the King County Rescue team board the two Locke boats and question the men on board. Dalton climbed onto the boat and collapsed on his back, gasping for breath. He looked up at Agents Carter and Munno, and the bald guy who were all raising their hands in surrender.

Dalton sat up and spotted his brother aiming a gun at the bald bastard who'd tried to escape.

"You want to handle this?" Carter asked Dalton.

Dalton stood. "Nate? What are you doing, buddy?"

"He's going to finally be a man. Go on, kid, shoot me," the bald guy taunted.

Nate's hand shook as he aimed the gun.

"This isn't you, kid. You don't kill people," Dalton said.

"They do. Why shouldn't I? They killed her," he croaked. "They killed Sydney."

"No, buddy. That's not true. Syd is fine."

Nate's gaze drifted from the bald guy to Dalton. What Dalton saw there scared the hell out of him. This was not his genius, naive brother.

"They killed her, Dalton. I saw the blood."

"Mind games, Nate. Look, I can prove it." He grabbed Carter's radio.

"Syd? I've got Nate. I need you to tell him you're alive and waiting to see him."

"Nathaniel? It's Sydney. I'm okay."

Nate's eyes filled with tears. "No, I saw…"

"I'm okay, Nate. Everything's okay now," Sydney said.

"It's a trick!" Nate screamed, closing one eye for a better aim at the bald guy.

"Keen," Carter warned Dalton.

"Keep talking, Syd," Dalton said.

"Nathaniel, it's really me," her sweet voice echoed over the radio. "You've got to come home because you promised to take me to see the new *X-Men* movie and I've been re-watching all the old movies and I have a new theory about Professor Xavier that I've been dying to tell you."

Dalton figured she was rambling because she was nervous and because she wanted to keep Nate grounded. It was working.

"Nathaniel? Stormie misses you," she continued. "She misses clawing up your pant leg and dive-bombing you on the sofa while you eat popcorn, and drinking your Hi-C juice and…and she misses curling up against your neck."

Nate blinked again, slower this time, and Dalton recognized exhaustion in his brother's eyes. Dalton lunged forward and caught Nate as he went down, the gun slipping from his fingers to the deck.

Nate's eyes blinked open, then closed.

"What's he on?" Dalton asked the bald prisoner.

"Nothing."

"Tell me!"

"We didn't drug him. He's broken because he's naive and weak."

Dalton sprung to his feet and backhanded the guy across the face.

"Easy." Carter placed a hand to Dalton's chest to keep him from killing the bastard. "I've got this guy. You take care of your brother."

Dalton knelt beside his brother and cradled his head in his lap. "Hey, buddy, it's okay now. Everything's going to be fine."

"I recognized the numbers on the chip," Nate said. "I called you."

"I know, man. I screwed up."

Nate scrunched up his face as if fighting off physical pain.

"What, Nate, where does it hurt?"

Then Dalton noticed the burned flesh of his arm and wanted to kill something.

Nate blinked and looked at Dalton. "Evidence…in *X-Men* DVD case."

"I know, buddy. We found it. You're a genius, kid."

"Dalton?" Nate asked.

He looked at his brave and beaten brother.

"Syd…is really okay?"

"She's great."

Nate closed his eyes and fell unconscious.

Chapter Sixteen

Sydney knew that something had changed. Her first clue was when Dalton didn't make eye contact, or share that boyish smile with her when she caught up with him at the hospital.

"How is he?" she asked, joining him in the waiting area.

"Good, considering what he's been through. They're moving him to a room."

He studied a stack of magazines.

She sat next to him. "Give it up."

"What?" He eyed her, but there was no warmth in his turquoise eyes, no tenderness.

"Something's wrong."

"My brother almost died. I'm messed up."

"Uh, not buying it."

"What do you want from me?" He stood and paced a few steps away.

"I want to know what happened between last night and now."

He turned to her. "What happened is I rescued my brother from hell, barely."

"Thanks to me."

"Fine, thank you, okay? You happy?"

"What's wrong with you?" She stood, but he put out his hand to keep her away.

"I've finally grown a conscience," he said.

"Excuse me?"

"My whole life it's been about me, my needs, my personal glory. Well, not this time. Nate needs you." He paused. "More than I do."

"Nate is my friend," she said. "That's all."

"He wanted to die because he thought you were dead. He would have committed murder to avenge you. He loves you."

"But I don't love him. Not like that."

"Gee-sus, woman, he's a great guy. He's smart and loyal and honest."

"But I love you."

He sighed and glanced at the ceiling. "I told you last night I couldn't make any promises."

"Until this case was resolved and now it's resolved."

"The resolution is that my brother needs you to help him recover. I won't do anything to screw that up. Hell, I've screwed up enough."

She clenched her jaw. She couldn't get through to him, not as long as he hid behind a shield of guilt and duty.

As much as her heart was breaking, it ached more for Dalton, a man who would never allow himself to be happy and content because he felt he didn't deserve it.

Baloney. He deserved happiness and so did Syd. But she wouldn't convince him of that right now, not while his brother lay broken in a hospital bed.

"You know what, Dalton?" She sauntered up to him and planted her hands to her hips. "I think I'd do more good comforting your brother than standing here arguing with you, you know why?"

He clenched his jaw, not answering.

"Because I don't have the energy to bang away at the armor you've got locked across your chest. When you're ready to stop hiding behind it, you come find me." She brushed past him and headed for the nurse's station to inquire about Nate.

Agent Carter stepped up beside her. "Ms. Trent?"

"What do you want?"

"I need to have a word with you."

"Not now.

"Bad time?"

"The worst."

"I'm sorry to hear that. I need to discuss the details of your future and thought if you had a minute."

"I need to see Nathaniel."

"They're settling him into his room now. It will be a few minutes before he's ready for visitors."

"Fine, so what's the plan? Am I going into witness protection or something?"

"That's one option. Another is…ever think about getting paid to use those decoding skills of yours?"

"Huh?"

"You're good with puzzles, figuring things out. My boss wanted me to mention a job opening with our organization."

"Me? A spy?"

"They don't call us that."

"No, they call you crazy," she muttered.

"Excuse me?"

"Never mind."

"If you're interested, we've got an assignment for a male-female team. It includes travel, all expenses paid."

"Ah. You did research on me and discovered my Achilles' heel."

He smiled. "We're short on female agents in our group and could use your help. Will you think about it?"

"Okay." She tapped her forefinger to her chin. "Do I get to pick my male partner?"

He raised a brow. "You mean, Dalton Keen?"

She nodded.

"I'll see what I can do."

A nurse approached them. "Sir, Mr. Keen is awake."

Carter nodded at Syd. "Why don't you go first?"

"Thanks."

Following the nurse into Nathaniel's room, she steeled herself against what she might see there. She didn't want to think about what they'd done to Nathaniel in the days he'd been held prisoner.

When she entered the room, she remarked that he looked surprisingly okay, although dwarfed by the starched sheets tucked around his body.

"He asked me to tuck him in tight because he's cold." The nurse looked at Syd. "His temperature is normal, blood pressure is fine."

Syd got the message. Nathaniel was cold, but there was no physical reason for the chill.

She went to his bedside and brushed copper-colored bangs off his forehead. He opened his eyes. For a second she didn't think he recognized her.

"Hey, Nathaniel. It's me, Syd."

He blinked, twice. "I know. Hi."

"It's really good to see you."

She kissed him on the forehead and stepped back. Her breath caught in her chest at the haunted look in his eyes. What did those bastards do to him?

"Don't worry," she said, pulling a chair close and sandwiching his hand between hers. "You're going to be okay."

"Are you?"

He seemed different today, older.

"What do you mean?" she asked.

"I can tell you're upset."

"I've been worried about you."

"No, it's something else."

"It's nothing. Your brother and I had a fight. Jerk," she muttered.

He cocked his head to the side. "Syd? You're in love with him, aren't you?"

"What, that bossy bruiser?"

"You've never been able to lie to me, Sydney."

"I've never wanted to lie to you."

"Then don't start now."

She sighed and stroked his hand. She noticed his other arm was wrapped in a white bandage from his wrist to his upper arm.

"When you disappeared, well, it was a mess," she said. "Dalton and I were so worried about you, and then they blew up your car and Dalton thought you were dead and—"

"You don't have to explain."

Who was this man? He surely wasn't her playful friend who drizzled chocolate on his popcorn and watched super hero movies with her.

"It doesn't matter," she said. "He's leaving, going to be reassigned."

"Does he love you?"

"He's not capable of love."

He shot her a scolding look. "Syd."

"He says I belong with you, because you need me."

He blinked and slipped his hand from hers. "What I need is to be left alone."

She wasn't sure she could stand being rejected by both Keen brothers in the course of an hour. "Nathaniel?"

"What?"

"You want me to leave?"

"Yes." He glanced up and she stilled at the intensity of his eyes. "We're officially over, Syd. I'm breaking off our engagement."

She thought she glimpsed his teasing, crooked smile, but it passed so quickly she couldn't be sure.

"Go on," he said. "Go help my brother."

Her heart warmed with the realization of what he was doing. Nate was opening the door for her and Dalton to be together.

"I need to sleep." Nate rolled over.

Syd placed her hand on his shoulder and whispered in his ear. "My theory on Professor Xavier? He is immortal." She paused. "And you…you are my hero."

DALTON FELT LIKE A caged panther desperate to make a kill. He needed out, damn it, out and away from Seattle.

Away from Syd.

Once he was back in the field, he'd be back to his old self, focused on rescuing innocents.

He paced from one end of the hotel room to the other. What dream world was he living in? Andrews was probably sending over paperwork for his termination.

Then what? He wondered where Syd was off to, what she planned to do with her life, and if there could be room for him.

Nope, don't go there. You will not betray your brother by stealing the love of his life. He saw it in Nate's eyes when he pointed the gun at the man he thought responsible for Syd's death. Nate was ready to kill and go to prison in the name of love.

Dalton was ready to go to hell. Yeah, that's where he'd be for the rest of his life, knowing that he could never be with the woman he loved because she belonged with his baby brother.

Which meant Dalton would lose Nate yet again because being around them, the two of them, would be too damn hard.

The hotel room door swung open and Agent Carter came in carrying bags of take-out food. "Hope you like Mexican."

"Sure, why not?" he said. Hell, he couldn't eat. Not until he was away from here.

He took one of the bags from Carter. "Is this where you give me my pink slip?"

Carter placed the other bag to the table. "Actually, Andrews was impressed that you kept a cool head, talked your brother out of the weapon and kept the suspect."

"I'm not out of a job?"

"No, actually, but, well, you'd better sit down for this."

"What?"

"Andrews is teaming you with a partner. And before you give me the line about working alone, remember you could be out of a job altogether."

"Good point."

"I stopped in to see your brother this morning," he said, pulling out a foil tray and removing the top.

"How is he?"

"Didn't you see him?"

"Not this morning. I…" His voice trailed off. What could he say? Confess that he was so damn ashamed of involving him in this that the guilt felt like a knife to his chest every time he saw his emotionally and physically scarred brother?

"He's a smart kid," Carter said. "He suspected something illegal was going on months before you asked for his help with the microchip case. He'd been keeping a log of Internet activity and odd occurrences, burned it to a CD, and put it in the DVD case so no one would find it. Then he got a look at the micro-chip and recognized a code used at work. Figured out Locke manufactured the chip, but once we got hold of it, Locke's people needed another way in, so they borrowed your brother."

"You mean, he was onto something before—"

"Before you asked for his help." He motioned to the container of food. "Sit. Eat. You look like hell."

Dalton absently opened a container.

"Anyway," Carter said, "your brother is brilliant but temporarily broken. Andrews is thinking we should at least keep an eye on him, and possibly offer him a job."

"Bad idea. He's too fragile."

Carter eyed him. "Some thought you were too fragile after your last mission."

"Yeah, well, my baby brother isn't me. He can't recover like me. He's naive and trusting and—"

"Are we talking about the same guy? I spent an hour with him this morning and he seemed tough."

Dalton couldn't get his head around it. "Nate? An agent? I can't see it."

"We could use a genius like him on our team. Hell, he broke into the government's mainframe and left a trail of breadcrumbs so the Feds could trace the source. Then he did some funky thing that broke the connection after fifteen minutes so Locke's team couldn't do too much damage."

But they'd done plenty of damage to Nate. Dalton had to look out for his baby brother now, more than ever.

Dalton stood. "I've got to see him."

"Make it quick. I need to debrief you."

Dalton left the hotel room for the hospital. What was he going to say to convince the kid to decline the job offer? Joining AW-21 would put his life in danger and Dalton couldn't protect him, especially if they were assigned to opposite ends of the world. Then again, if Nate was stuck in an office in Virginia, he couldn't get into too much trouble.

He made it to the hospital in less than ten minutes, parked and went to Nate's room. His brother was struggling to get out of bed.

"Hey, buddy, you sure you should be doing that?" Dalton raced to his side and grabbed his arm for support.

Nate wrenched away. "Let go of me."

"You need to stay in bed, kid."

Nate leveled him with angry green eyes. "I'm not a kid and I don't take orders from you."

Dalton was stunned by the tone of his brother's voice.

"Nate, I'm sorry. I'm trying to help."

"Don't. I'll be fine." He sucked in a deep breath to fight back the pain.

"You want me to get the nurse?" Dalton asked.

"No, I want you to leave me alone. You and Sydney need to leave me the hell alone so I can get on with my life."

Dalton leaned against the wall and crossed his arms over his chest. "And what are you going to do with your life?"

"I'm not sure yet."

"But you're not going to join my organization, right?"

Nate glared at him. "You got a problem with that?"

"Yes."

"Why, because I'm not big and strong like you? Because I'm a weak geek?"

"No, because you're my brother and I don't want to see you hurt."

"Kind of late for that."

His remark felt like a knife had been plunged into Dalton's heart. "Nate, I'm sorry."

"Don't be." Nate stood, suddenly, as if he didn't struggle against a weakened body and battered psyche.

Dalton could tell the mental torture had been as ruthless as the physical. He wanted to reach out to Nate but didn't dare.

Nate shuffled to the window. "This was the best thing that could have happened to me. It forced me to grow up, stand on my own, which means I need you to get the hell out of my life."

"Nate." He touched the kid's shoulder and Nate batted his hand away.

"Don't. I need you to leave," Nate said, his voice trembling. "Please."

Dalton's chest ached as he walked to the door trying to figure out what words could fix this situation.

"Dalton?" Nate said.

Dalton turned but Nate was staring out the window. "Stop beating yourself up," Nate offered. "If you keep doing that, you're letting him win."

Him, their father, the man who'd tried so hard to break his boys because of his own insecurities and fears.

"I'm moving on." Nate turned to face him. "It's time you did the same."

"I love you, Nate." There, he said it, didn't know how the words came out of his mouth, and he didn't dare do what he wanted to do which was hug his brother.

Nate glanced back out the window.

Dalton took his cue to leave and headed for the hotel, struggling to figure out whom he'd just spoken to, because the wise soul offering Dalton absolution didn't resemble his kid brother.

Torture changed a person. It had taught Dalton not to give up, nor to trust anyone ever again.

Except somehow, against his better judgment and his will, Ms. Sydney Trent had ripped that resolution to shreds. She'd eased her way into Dalton's heart and settled there, offering him love and compassion.

He couldn't accept it. And that was tearing him apart.

He made it back to the hotel so he could finish the debrief and get his next assignment.

A partner? Hell. He couldn't process that right now, still raw from his conversation with Nate. Nate needed distance? Okay, fine. Dalton would respect his wishes, for now.

Dalton let himself into the hotel room. "Let's get this over with," he said to Carter, then froze at the sight of Sydney standing by the window.

"What's she doing here?" he demanded.

"*She* has a name, jerk," she shot back.

"I have to debrief both of you before I start my next assignment but I've got someone waiting downstairs," Carter said. "Can you two play nice for a few minutes?"

"I can," Syd said. "I'm a *mature* person."

She sat down and shifted the cat carrier onto her lap.

"Behave," Carter said to Dalton, leaving them alone.

Dalton sat on the edge of the bed, fighting back the memories of the love they'd shared in this very room.

"How's Storm?" he asked.

"Cranky. She wants to go home."

"Where's…home?"

"I don't know yet."

"You're not leaving the area, are you? I mean, my brother needs his friends around."

"Your brother?" She stared him down. "He told me to get lost. I had the pleasure of experiencing two rejections from the Keen brothers in the same day."

"But I thought—"

"Look, Nate and I were never romantically involved. I've told you that a gazillion times. He was freaked out when he thought they'd killed me, sure, but he'd been emotionally and physically abused for days and I was his best friend, and

Drew had been killed and Nate blamed himself and he couldn't stand the thought of me being hurt because of him."

She was utterly adorable when she rambled. And that's when he knew he couldn't live without this fantastic woman in his life.

"You did all that in one breath," he remarked.

She pointed her finger at him. "Do not tease me. You've lost that right."

He sighed. "I'm sorry."

"You're in love with me and you passed me off to your brother!"

"I felt guilty that I'd stolen you from him."

"I was never his to steal."

"Even so, I was ashamed that I did it again. I put my needs first, and stole the love of his life. I didn't take care of him."

"You jumped into the frigid lake and saved him. If you can't see how that is taking care of him, well…then maybe I don't want to be partnered with a dumb-as-rocks jock."

"Partnered?"

"Your bosses were impressed that I could figure out stuff their experts couldn't, thanks to my poster board art. It seems they have an opening in your organization for a male-female team. And I get to pick my male."

He took her hand. "Sydney, I don't want you in that kind of danger."

She snapped it back. "Hey, in case you've forgotten, I'm pretty good at taking care of myself. That's more than I can say for you, Mr. Turn-my-back-on-love Keen."

"I don't deserve it," he blurted out.

"What?" she hushed.

He closed his eyes. "You heard me."

"You take that back or I'm going to sick Storm on you." She unlocked the cat carrier.

"I don't know how…to deserve it," he whispered.

She put the carrier on the table and sat beside Dalton. She placed an open palm to his cheek and he thought he'd fall apart.

"That's why you've got me," she said. "To remind you every single day how much you deserve to be happy, how much *we* deserve to be happy. Together."

He didn't feel like he deserved this woman, but he trusted her. If she said they deserved happiness, then they must.

"Together," she repeated.

"I like that word." He brushed a strand of blond hair from her cheek.

"And I like you." She leaned forward and kissed him.

His heart filled with love. This wasn't just his new work partner, but Syd was his life partner. For once the anxious stirring of his conscience quieted to a hum of contentment.

Dalton held his love in his arms and realized he *did* deserve her, every delicious inch of her, body and soul.

* * * * *

Eight years ago Matt Shaffer had vanished out of Natalie Rothchild's life, leaving behind a one-line note tucked under a pillow that had grown cold: *I'm sorry, but this just isn't going to work.*

That was it. No explanation, no real indication of remorse. The note had been as clinical and compassionless as an eviction notice, which, in effect, it had been, Natalie thought as she navigated through the morning traffic. Matt had written the note to evict her from his life.

She'd spent the next two weeks crying, breaking down without warning as she walked down the street, or as she sat staring at a meal she couldn't bring herself to eat.

Candace, she remembered with a bittersweet pang, had tried to get her to go clubbing in order to get her to forget about Matt.

She'd turned her twin down, but she did get her act together. If Matt didn't think enough of their relationship to try to contact her, to try to make her understand why he'd changed so radically from lover to stranger, then to hell with him. He was dead to her, she resolved. And he'd remained that way.

Until twenty minutes ago.

The adrenaline in her veins kept mounting.

Natalie focused on her driving. Vegas in the daylight wasn't nearly as alluring, as magical and glitzy as it was after dark. Like an aging woman best seen in soft lighting, Vegas's imperfections were all visible in the daylight. Natalie supposed that was why people like her sister didn't like to get up until noon. They lived for the night.

Except that Candace could no longer do that.

The thought brought a fresh, sharp ache with it.

"Damn it, Candy, what a waste," Natalie murmured under her breath.

She pulled up before the Janus casino. One of the three valets currently on duty came to life and made a beeline for her vehicle.

"Welcome to the Janus," the young attendant said cheerfully as he opened her door with a flourish.

"We'll see," she replied solemnly.

As he pulled away with her car, Natalie looked up at the casino's logo. Janus was the Roman god with two faces, one pointed toward the past, the other facing the future. It struck her as rather ironic, given what she was doing here, seeking out someone from her past in order to get answers so that the future could be settled.

The moment she entered the casino, the Vegas phenomena took hold. It was like stepping into a world where time did not matter or even make an appearance. There was only a sense of "now."

Because in Natalie's experience she'd discovered that bartenders knew the inner workings of any establishment they worked for better than anyone else, she made her way to the first bar she saw within the casino.

The bartender in attendance was a gregarious man in his early forties. He had a quick, sexy smile, which was probably one of the main reasons he'd been hired. His name tag identified him as Kevin.

Moving to her end of the bar, Kevin asked, "What'll it be, pretty lady?"

"Information." She saw a dubious look cross his brow. To counter that, she took out her badge. Granted she wasn't here in an official capacity, but Kevin didn't need to know that. "Were you on duty last night?"

Kevin began to wipe the gleaming black surface of the bar. "You mean during the gala?"

"Yes."

The smile gracing his lips was a satisfied one. Last night had obviously been profitable for him, she judged. "I caught an extra shift."

She took out Candace's photograph and carefully placed it on the bar. "Did you happen to see this woman there?"

The bartender glanced at the picture. Mild interest turned to recognition. "You mean Candace Rothchild? Yeah, she was here, loud and brassy as always. But not for long," he added, looking rather disappointed. There was always a circus when Candace was around, Natalie thought. "She and the boss had at it and then he had our head of security escort her out."

She latched on to the first part of his statement. "They argued? About what?"

He shook his head. "Couldn't tell you. Too far away for anything but body language," he confessed.

"And the head of security?" she asked.

"He got her to leave."

She leaned in over the bar. "Tell me about him."

"Don't know much," the bartender admitted. "Just that his name's Matt Shaffer. Boss flew him in from L.A., where he was head of security for Montgomery Enterprises."

There was no avoiding it, she thought darkly. She was going to have to talk to Matt. The thought left her cold. "Do you know where I can find him right now?"

Kevin glanced at his watch. "He should be in his office. On the second floor, toward the rear." He gave her the numbers of the rooms where the monitors that kept watch over the casino guests as they tried their luck against the house were located.

Taking out a twenty, she placed it on the bar. "Thanks for your help."

Kevin slipped the bill into his vest pocket. "Any time, lovely lady," he called after her. "Any time."

She debated going up the stairs, then decided on the elevator. The car that took her up to the second floor was empty. Natalie stepped out of the elevator, looked around to get her bearings and then walked toward the rear of the floor.

"Into the Valley of Death rode the six hundred," she silently recited, digging deep for a line from a poem by Tennyson. Wrapping her hand around a brass handle, she opened one of the glass doors and walked in.

The woman whose desk was closest to the door looked up. "You can't come in here. This is a restricted area."

Natalie already had her ID in her hand and held it up. "I'm looking for Matt Shaffer," she told the woman.

God, even saying his name made her mouth go dry. She was supposed to be over him, to have moved on with her life. What happened?

The woman began to answer her. "He's—"

"Right here."

The deep voice came from behind her. Natalie felt every single nerve ending go on tactical alert at the same moment that all the hairs at the back of her neck stood up. Eight years had passed, but she would have recognized his voice anywhere.

* * * * *

*Why did Matt Shaffer leave heiress-turned-cop
Natalie Rothchild?
What does he know about the death of
Natalie's twin sister?
Come and meet these two reunited lovers and learn the
secrets of the Rothchild family in
THE HEIRESS'S 2-WEEK AFFAIR
by* USA TODAY *bestselling author
Marie Ferrarella.
The first book in Silhouette® Romantic Suspense's wildly
romantic new continuity,*
LOVE IN 60 SECONDS!
Available April 2009.

CELEBRATE
60 YEARS
OF PURE READING PLEASURE
WITH **HARLEQUIN**®!

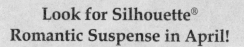

Look for Silhouette®
Romantic Suspense in April!

Love In 60 Seconds

Bright lights. Big city. Hearts in overdrive.

Silhouette® Romantic Suspense is celebrating Harlequin's 60th Anniversary with six stories that promise to bring readers the glitz of Las Vegas, the danger of revenge, the mystery of a missing diamond, and family scandals.

Look for the first title, *The Heiress's 2-Week Affair* by *USA TODAY* bestselling author Marie Ferrarella, on sale in April!

His 7-Day Fiancée by **Gail Barrett**	May
The 9-Month Bodyguard by **Cindy Dees**	June
Prince Charming for 1 Night by **Nina Bruhns**	July
Her 24-Hour Protector by **Loreth Anne White**	August
5 minutes to Marriage by **Carla Cassidy**	September

Undone!

THE RAKE'S INHERITED COURTESAN
Ann Lethbridge

Christopher Evernden has been assigned the unfortunate task of minding Parisian courtesan Sylvia Boisette. When Syliva sets off to find her father, Christopher has no choice but to follow and finds her kidnapped by an Irishman. Once rescued, they finally succumb to the temptation that has been brewing between them. But can they see past the limitations such a love can bring?

Available April 2009
wherever books are sold.

The Inside Romance newsletter has a NEW look for the new year!

Same great content, brand-new look!

The Inside Romance newsletter is a FREE quarterly newsletter highlighting our upcoming series releases and promotions!

Click on the Inside Romance link on the front page of **www.eHarlequin.com** or e-mail us at insideromance@harlequin.ca to sign up to receive your FREE newsletter today!

You can also subscribe by writing to us at: HARLEQUIN BOOKS Attention: Customer Service Department P.O. Box 9057, Buffalo, NY 14269-9057

Please allow 4-6 weeks for delivery of the first issue by mail.

IRNNEW09

REQUEST YOUR FREE BOOKS!

2 FREE NOVELS
PLUS 2
FREE GIFTS!

⊕ HARLEQUIN®

INTRIGUE®

Breathtaking Romantic Suspense

YES! Please send me 2 FREE Harlequin Intrigue® novels and my 2 FREE gifts (gifts are worth about $10). After receiving them, if I don't wish to receive any more books, I can return the shipping statement marked "cancel." If I don't cancel, I will receive 6 brand-new novels every month and be billed just $4.24 per book in the U.S. or $4.99 per book in Canada. That's a savings of close to 15% off the cover price! It's quite a bargain! Shipping and handling is just 25¢ per book*. I understand that accepting the 2 free books and gifts places me under no obligation to buy anything. I can always return a shipment and cancel at any time. Even if I never buy another book from Harlequin, the two free books and gifts are mine to keep forever.

182 HDN EEZ7   382 HDN EEZK

Name	(PLEASE PRINT)	
Address		Apt. #
City	State/Prov.	Zip/Postal Code

Signature (if under 18, a parent or guardian must sign)

Mail to the **Harlequin Reader Service:**
IN U.S.A.: P.O. Box 1867, Buffalo, NY 14240-1867
IN CANADA: P.O. Box 609, Fort Erie, Ontario L2A 5X3

Not valid to current subscribers of Harlequin Intrigue books.

**Are you a current subscriber of Harlequin Intrigue books
and want to receive the larger-print edition?
Call 1-800-873-8635 today!**

* Terms and prices subject to change without notice. Prices do not include applicable taxes. Sales tax applicable in N.Y. Canadian residents will be charged applicable provincial taxes and GST. Offer not valid in Quebec. This offer is limited to one order per household. All orders subject to approval. Credit or debit balances in a customer's account(s) may be offset by any other outstanding balance owed by or to the customer. Please allow 4 to 6 weeks for delivery. Offer available while quantities last.

Your Privacy: Harlequin is committed to protecting your privacy. Our Privacy Policy is available online at www.eHarlequin.com or upon request from the Reader Service. From time to time we make our lists of customers available to reputable third parties who may have a product or service of interest to you. If you would prefer we not share your name and address, please check here. ☐

HI09

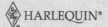
INTRIGUE

COMING NEXT MONTH

Available April 14, 2009

#1125 SHOTGUN BRIDE by B.J. Daniels
Whitehorse, Montana: The Corbetts
A former Texas Ranger is not prepared to fall for a blue-eyed Montana cowgirl who has had enough of heartbreak. When her troubling past leads to her abduction, is he ready to ride to her rescue?

#1126 CRIMINALLY HANDSOME by Cassie Miles
Kenner County Crime Unit
A terrifying vision sends a frightened psychic into the protective arms of a skeptical CSI expert. To catch a killer, they will need to work together—closely.

#1127 BABY BLING by Elle James
Diamonds and Daddies
Two months ago, Houston's shipping tycoon slept with the one woman he should have left alone—his assistant and friend. Now he needs her help to stop terrorists, and she needs to tell him she is pregnant!

#1128 RESCUING THE VIRGIN by Patricia Rosemoor
The McKenna Legacy
An undercover special agent is shocked when he discovers a beautiful American woman trapped by the human-trafficking ring he is trying to bring down. Can he save her and bring the mastermind behind the scheme to justice?

#1129 A STRANGER'S BABY by Kerry Connor
With the help of the handsome man next door, she is unraveling the sinister truth behind the one-night stand that left her pregnant and alone. Now that someone is threatening her baby and safety, can they find out the truth before it is too late?

#1130 BULLETPROOF TEXAS by Kay Thomas
To extract cancer-eating bacteria from a flooding cave, a research scientist accepts the help of a laid-back caving guide. But a psychopathic competitor decides this potential cure shouldn't see the light of day—and is willing to kill anyone who gets in the way.

HICNMBPA0309